Assessing Survival
Mechanical Advantage 1

By

Viola Grace

In the year 2280, Earth has been at war for a decade. The Splice take the humans they capture and use them for parts. Sending bots in place of humans didn't work, but taking the wounded and turning them into cyborgs has enabled Earth to push the Splice away from Earth. The combination of metal and man is turning the tide in a war that no one could have imagined.

Adaptation Base is where the wounded are recycled into enhanced warriors, and when a terrorist action takes out the administration, the newest cyborgs will have to take things into their own hands.

When Stitch comes to, her position as an assessment officer is still valid, but her new location on the front lines means a lot of adjustment. The men she had designed from the wounds out are now her team, and finding the one who had flirted his way into her heart—after all this time—leaves her vulnerable to his mechanical advantage.

Chapter One

Stitch stroked her patient's hair back from his face, moving her hand as the scanner reached his head. The moment she could, she began the soothing touch again.

Her handheld terminal chirped when she got the scan results. "Sit tight, Private Matthews. I will see what we can do for you."

His bright blue eyes had a colour that was startling in the ravaged expanse of his face.

His eyes were the only part of his face that was still intact. It was a miracle in and of itself. Most of the patients coming through had ocular damage.

"Rest easy. Let the painkillers do their work, and I will be back as soon as I have consulted with the doctors."

He closed and opened his eyes slowly.

"I will take that as a yes. Don't worry. You will live through this and come out on the other side."

He closed his eyes and a tear trickled down his temple. She smiled softly and stroked his hair again. "Let us make you whole again."

The nurse moved in and sedated him.

Stitch turned and headed to the conference room, where six doctors were on screens, ready to weigh in on the cyber modifications that Private Matthews was about to undergo.

Stitch settled in her chair and sat up straight. "Doctors, we have before you the case of Private Matthews. He has facial trauma. His left arm was harvested, and his right was crushed. There is damage to his torso that requires skin grafts and more damage to his lower extremities that cannot be repaired via the nanites."

She tapped the file on her screen. "Now, tell me how we can put him back together and make it good."

Stitch sat back and listened to the doctors discuss the available options. Arm and limb replacements were discussed. His jaw would have to be encapsulated while the nanites did their slow repair job.

She mentally thanked the egotists who used the nanites as medical care over the last century. The tiny robots made the cyborg program possible, and the cyborgs were making incredible strides in the war.

The Splice had attacked the space stations at first and then moved on to the first human colony. They didn't want minerals or oxygen or any part of the world they landed on. They wanted the biological materials of their enemies to add to their own fused systems.

Humanity had thrown themselves at the intruders in their space and had been soundly beaten. When the battle-damaged started coming home, an ancient technology saved them. The doctors used the cybernetic implants and built warriors with weapons that stood a chance against their opponents and could not be taken from them.

In the previous century, those who were inclined used the nanite technology to fuse the metal to their skin and bone. It was a cosmetic freak show that had grown tiresome in a decade. Now, they were using that same tech to fuse weapons to flesh to remake wounded warriors into weapons once again.

With only one out of a hundred men

making it back from the border that humanity was trying to defend, sending those who survived back into battle was their best bet.

Private Matthews had signed a reconstruction authorization, as had ninety percent of those who went into battle against the Splice.

When the doctors finally began to list solid points for connection, Stitch assembled the necessary components for the adaptation, and Matthews's virtual scans began to take on the cybernetic components.

As the last of the possible components were added to the projection, she thanked the council of physicians.

"Your service to your world is appreciated. When the adaptation is complete, you will be sent copies of the medical files for your own perusal."

The doctors thanked her, and the

screens went blank.

Stitch called in the engineering officers on duty, as well as the transplant specialists and cyber mechanics. They all came from different parts of the station and began to work on the feasibility of the additions.

Cracker and Lucky were with the others. Lucky was looking at the cranial scans and judging the space left in his skull to implant control modules. Programming for all the limbs needed a solid place to work from. Closer to the spine was better. Using the body's nervous system to relay the information meant they didn't have to put in wires to do the work.

Cracker was checking the multitude of additions and nixing all but a basic few. The engineers fought her, but she stood firm.

"When they need maintenance, and

they do, hiding those ports, jacks and servo systems under tissue drastically reduces the possibility of a fast repair and expedited turnaround. Keep it simple, make everything a multitasker, and get him up and running as quickly as possible."

Stitch piped up. "Don't forget his voice. He needs his voice back."

Cracker grimaced and put the vocal enhancements back in place. "I have yet to meet a man whose voice was worth listening to."

Lucky smirked, "You are hanging around with the wrong men."

The other men in the room looked offended. They were older and unfit for duty on the border. Many of them had grandsons on the front lines. Most had lost someone.

For hours, they redesigned Matthews, until finally, they had something that would enable him to enjoy the life that had been returned to him as well as the power that would make him into a living weapon.

"Do we have a consensus?"

Stitch looked at every face in the room. The recordings were still active.

"Aye." Six voices spoke at once.

With a few flicks of her fingers, she sent a copy of the file to the supply office, the equipment locker and the medical team. The pattern was set. They just had to put everything into place.

Acknowledgements came from each department, and Stitch sighed in relief.

"Procedure is confirmed and underway. Broadcast of progress will be forwarded after Matthews is on the road to recovery."

She turned off the recording modules and got to her feet, stretching and twisting. The specialists on the main floor looked up at her, and she nodded. "Get to it. We need him back in action by the end of the week."

Lucky was waiting at the base of the stairs that led up to the crow's nest that let Stitch communicate and monitor everything regarding the design.

"So, are you coming tonight?"

Stitch chuckled. "Of course. We have the private room off the mess hall. We can have as much fun as is allowed by Extra-Earth policies."

"You know how much that fun is?"

Stitch shrugged. "Ask Alphy. She knows everything."

Lucky grinned. "I am sure she will tell us if we get out of hand."

"Without us even asking." Stitch gave her a one-armed hug. "Well, go and set-up the control modules for Matthews. He has a lot of potential."

"Off I go." Lucky headed for the door,

bumped into it and then righted herself to continue onward.

Stitch wondered how her friend had made it through life without countless breaks and major damage, but she always managed to skate through with only light bruising and a cheeky grin.

With her duty to Matthews completed, she headed back to the med bay and sat with him as he was prepped for surgery. He looked at her, and his eyes were calm.

"Don't worry, Matthews; when you wake up, you will be able to speak again and your recovery will speed past."

He blinked slowly, the pure blue eyes clear and understanding.

The docs came for him, and she pressed a kiss to his forehead before he left.

She watched him go, knowing that the nanites would repair his skin and muscle eventually, but when the implants were set in place, the little bots would graft him to the metal. Lucky's programming would see to that.

She checked her schedule, and there was nothing left for her to do until the next medivac came to the station.

Only a dozen survivors had been on the last flight. There were more than twelve bays to redesign the warriors, but they went unused.

Stitch returned to her office and filed her reports. It always felt odd to sign her whole name, but *Assessment Officer Stephanie S. Carter* had to appear at the bottom of every report.

She checked the chronometer and kept working. Five hours until the party. She might just finish the paperwork on time.

Stitch watched as Lucky opened another parcel from the assembled ladies.

The newest member of their group smiled shyly as Lucky opened the box. Twenty girls laughed and gasped as the silky lingerie was put on display.

Lucky gasped and shoved it back in the box. "I am not going to wear that."

The supply officer, Lacey, smiled, "It is worth its weight in microchips. The silk was taken off a Splice ship and was brought back by one of the salvage teams. It was crafted on another world."

Lucky pulled it out again, and Stitch smirked. Lacey had come in three months earlier and already had a reputation for getting anything you could want in a surprisingly short amount of time.

The girls all marvelled at the exotic nature of the gift.

When the gifts had all been handed over by the one who brought them, there was one package left.

There was something odd about the box. It was wrapped with gleaming paper and a big, floppy bow. It was so girly as to be a caricature of a gift for a lady. There was a note tag dangling from the box.

Lucky picked up the box and examined the bow. "Huh, it says, *From Your Secret Admirer.*"

Stitch was moving as Lucky tugged the tag free. She thought she screamed, "Get down!" but she couldn't be sure.

She tackled Lucky as the bomb in her hands exploded.

Stitch felt the searing pain in her back and her arm. She tried to move her right arm, but she couldn't. Lucky had blood streaming from her head, and her hands were scorched, her breathing was even and Stitch counted the breaths to make sure she was still functioning.

She leaned up on her left arm and looked around. Over half the women were dead and several more were on their way to it.

Cracker was next to the com and whispering, doing a head count of the survivors.

A moment later, there were medics streaming in and doing triage on the damaged ladies.

Half of the administration of the transformation and repair station had been wiped out in the explosion. This was definitely war.

Stitch grunted as the medics lifted her up. "Hey, Antony, Morry."

"Damn, Stitch. You are going to be one of your own patients." Antony tried to keep his gaze bright, but there was worry in it.

"Remind me to play poker with you,

Antony. You look extremely worried."

"Scans indicate shattered internal organs. You have blown your kidneys, and your spleen is ruptured. This is going to get worse before it gets better."

She nodded, and they settled her on a gurney. "Make sure that you check on Lucky. I am worried about a brain bleed."

"Yes, ma'am."

As they rushed her and the others down the hall, she lay back and spoke to Morry. "I need a full report on the survivors the moment that I make it out of triage."

"You aren't in any position to be giving orders, Stitch." Morry held her left hand as they were in the lift, heading for medical.

"I know, but I figured it doesn't hurt to try. How many made it?"

Antony cleared his throat. "Eight are

still alive, but we are expecting to lose two."

She watched as he stiffened. He was getting an update on his internal communicator. "We are down to six, including you. Don't make me redo the count, Stitch."

She chuckled and lay back; the pain wasn't too bad, but then, it wouldn't be with her spine broken and her body numb below the waist.

They hadn't mentioned it, but then, there had to be a reason that she wasn't feeling the pain of the crushing damaged caused by the blast.

When they arrived in medical, every staff member was on deck. She was moved from the gurney to the scanner, and she was subjected to the same treatment that she oversaw on a daily basis.

She felt the shock and insecurity that

came when others discussed her fate, and she had no say in it. She tried to offer her expert opinion, but they sedated her. It all went downhill from there.

Chapter Two

"Assessment Officer Carter, please move your toes."

Stitch didn't recognize the voice, but it didn't matter. She twitched her toes for him.

"Excellent. Well, you came through the adaptation just fine. You went into shipping shock. Glad to see you are with us."

She opened her eyes and looked around. It took her a few tries to speak. "Not the station."

The doctor working on her paused. "You are awake."

"You told me to move. Did you think I was sleeping?"

"No, I was counting on the processors to make your body move. I was using the master frequency."

He made eye contact with her, and she blinked as the features registered. "I know you. Captain Blue."

His dark-brown eyes warmed with pleased surprise. "Yes."

"Lung damage and a wounded leg. They replaced the leg, throat, vocal system and, of course, the lungs."

He was wearing black military garb and had a series of scanners at his disposal. The med scanners were battlefield issue, and Stitch had a very good idea of where she was.

He chuckled. "I am surprised. So many folks go through that station."

"I am at Alpha Base." She looked around and saw rows of beds, half filled.

"You are still excellent at assessment, I see. As the order forces all cyborgs to be on the front lines, you and the other survivors were shipped out to the stations and holding border outposts. It took some doing. Custom adaptations had to be created for each of you."

"A sizing problem, right?"

The captain pushed a button to raise her up into a sitting position.

Stitch lifted her hands to check her hair, and one of those hands was silver. "Well, that is different."

"They had to keep you in hibernation with your jacks in place while they waited for your adaptations to be assembled. You are wearing the most modern implants available."

"Kidneys, spleen, and any other organs?"

He nodded. "Your intestines managed to recover during your surgeries."

"Can I see my file?"

He nodded. "As you are taking over

our triage assessment team as soon as you are up and running, yes."

He handed her the flat screen, and she extended it out of the two cylinders. Her stats were displayed, and her new silver hand moved as easily as her flesh one while flicking through the information.

She had died twice, her system had gone septic and additional nanites had been injected to give her enough to be compatible with the adaptations, as well as bolster her immune system. Her broken spine had been fixed and the impulses from her body rerouted around the damage.

Major organs had been replaced with the newest and most organic implants available. She had been held in hibernation while they had built the parts. She had been out of commission for two years.

"What happened to the others?" She looked up at the captain.

"They are scattered across the front. You ladies have skills, and we need more fighters, as well as admin specialists."

"Did they find out who planted the bomb?"

"They did. It was the War Opposition Front—those idiots who wanted to hand over Earth and beg for mercy from the Splice. They didn't know that mercy would never be coming from that front."

"What has happened?"

"We sealed the Earth. A defense net of weaponized satellites was launched three months ago. It has repelled one Splice attack, but now, they are gathering in numbers. It won't be long before they crack through." He grimaced.

"What is being done about it?"

Captain Blue shrugged. "Whatever we can do. We are trying to cut them off."

Stitch nodded. "Great. When can I get out of bed?"

"As soon as you are ready. Sit with your legs over the side and slowly get up. If you feel weak, fall back. The bed is designed to hold fully tricked-out cyborgs. You won't even make it tremble."

He stayed near her while she moved her heavy legs to hang over the edge. It was difficult, but once her body knew what she wanted, it cooperated. She waited until she could swing her legs to her heartbeat, and when she was ready, she stood.

Her balance was off. They hadn't installed a counterweight along her left arm. Stitch twisted and slowly bent. When she straightened, she looked at Captain Blue. "Okay, where can I get some clothes?"

He stopped staring at her naked body and blinked. "Uh, in your quarters? We don't have a lot of call for clothing in your size."

"Find me a t-shirt, perv. I am not here to entertain you."

"I had to assess the connections."

"Yes, and now that is done and there is no medical reason to keep me in here anymore, I am not going to sprint through the halls like this."

The captain inclined his head and left her to get her a t-shirt.

Well, that is where Stitch hoped he was going. He could be leaving her on her own.

She flicked the screen out and went looking for her friends. Lucky, Lacey, Windy, Cracker and Alphy were all reported as on active medical leave. Their locations were not listed, but they were alive.

Stitch nodded and noted something amusing. Her rank was now that of major. She outranked the good captain, and he was hoping she didn't know it.

After their procedures, all cyborgs were promoted to sergeant or higher. Her rank must not have sunk in yet.

She checked on the investigation of the bombing, and the WOF had indeed claimed responsibility. Several members had been prosecuted, but it didn't answer the question that Stitch had. How had they gotten the bomb onto the station? Who had hated the girls enough to try and kill most of them in one shot?

She walked slowly down the hall with a man named Sergeant Trent escorting her. Half his face had been replaced with metal, and he had the easy gait of a long-time cyborg.

After five minutes of pacing silently, he said, "So, you are one of the survivors?"

"More or less. A dozen good women, skilled women, died that day. Part of me died with them." She was grim about it, but it was true. She hadn't had time to grieve, but it was coming.

"Your arm?" Trent gestured to the silver melded with her skin.

"My soul. I don't know where my friends are or what kind of shape they are in. It has been two years for the world, but for me, it was just a few hours ago."

"You have been out that whole time?"

"I have. I desperately need to brush my teeth, get dressed and find something to eat."

"I will wait outside your door and take you to the commissary when you are ready."

"Thank you, Sergeant."

"Call me George. You held my hand while we waited for me to be prepped for surgery. You even cried a little when I told you I was scared."

She had only cried for one patient. Her first. She turned to face him and looked into his human eye. "Oh my god. It is you."

She reached up and stroked the scar over his eyebrow and followed it as it curled down to the corner of his eye.

He chuckled. "I remember that touch. You fought for me to keep the eye, and for that, I thank you. The Splice might be able to fool sensors, but they can't fool human sight."

It had been her first fight with the doctors. They had wanted to put in a full ocular prosthetic set and call it a day. She had argued to keep whatever they could. His skin had been torn, but the nanites had sealed it. It was cosmetic damage.

She smiled. "I am glad that I helped

them to the right decision."

"As am I. Your quarters are this way, Major Carter."

She chuckled. "Call me Stitch. Everyone does."

They started moving down the corridor again. "You are Stitch? Seriously? I never put that together with the woman I met during my stay at the station."

"Put what together?"

"The guys who come from the station all have a crush on the woman named Stitch who stayed at their bedsides and fought to keep them as whole as was possible. That goes a long way with these guys. Many have family back home, and going back as a cyborg will be hard enough. The more of them that can stay human, the better."

"That was the theory I was operating under. We tried to give them the best mods with the most useful applications and enough to make them feel as normal as possible."

He nodded. "I know. How are you enjoying being on the other side of the process?"

"I wish I had had a Stitch of my own working with the team. I need a counterweight on my left side to balance the metal hand and forearm."

"They will be able to manage that here. Alpha Base is fairly well equipped for repairs."

She grimaced. "I want my team back. I don't know what my role is going to be here, but I know I want my team."

"You are going to have to make a new team. Yours is scattered across the system."

They were in the living quarters now and catching quite a few amazed glances. The guys might have known she was coming, but seeing her was a separate matter.

"These are your quarters. Alpha Base doesn't have separate rooms for females, so you are stuck with the guys. Don't worry. We all respect the role you are going to play at the base, Major Carter. I mean, Stitch."

"Yeah, I have been on bases before. Let's see how long that lasts." She had no illusions about what could happen if she let her guard down.

She looked for a way to open the door. "How does this work?"

"Oh, there is a bio scan. Step right up to the door."

Right, of course. There would be no way for half of the population to use a palm scanner, and even less could manage an ocular scan. Even breath was out of the question. Having the scanner compare them to their med files was the fastest way.

Her door hissed open, and it was like being back on the adaptation station. Her room was exactly as she left it. Her terminal was a little more advanced but in the same place. Someone had gone to a lot of trouble to make this feel like home.

"I will be out here when you are ready to get your meal." George nodded and turned his back to the closing door.

She found her private bathroom and pulled off the black t-shirt. Her shower was quick, but she felt better after it.

A series of uniforms had been added to her wardrobe. She supposed that she should put one on.

Her lingerie drawer had only been manhandled a little, and she put on her bra and panties before sliding on the black cargo pants, tank top and button-down shirt. The boots were a little clunky but nothing compared to the battle gear that the guys had to put on.

She straightened, brushed her hair and scrubbed her teeth.

Stitch fastened her hair back in a bun and headed to the door. Time to get started; she had slept long enough.

Chapter Three

The food at the base was just like the food at the station, but instead of the view of the stars, there was a huge planet looming above them.

Stitch could almost feel the pull of Jupiter and its hypnotic spot.

George sat across from her, and they ate their meals off stamped, metal trays.

Stitch's meal had appeared after she let the scanner check her identity. That was when she knew that there was a chip of some sort in the new hand.

"The scanners will only give you what your body can handle. You are lucky. You seem to be on a standard diet."

Stitch eyed the contents of her tray.

"If you call this luck."

She ate a few bites of what appeared to be stew that had already been chewed by someone. It didn't taste too bad, so she dove in with a little more enthusiasm. It was something she was willing to get used to. There wasn't really a choice.

Stitch made a list of things she needed to get done to her own body. As long as she was focused on something, the images of the party didn't rear up in her mind.

George was quiet while she ate, and when she got to her feet with her tray, he simply directed her down a hallway.

"We just had an incoming ship when you woke up. If you are feeling up to it, would you take on your duties?"

"Sure. As long as I can put in an order for my counterweight while I am there."

"Of course." He nodded.

"You have no clue, do you?"

George chuckled. "You still have skills at reading people, so that is good."

Stitch sighed and listened to the hollow thud of her boots on the deck plates. She could smell the recycled air, the metal everywhere and the unmistakable scent of men in every direction.

When she smelled blood, she knew they were close to the med centre.

She reached into her pocket and pulled out her com unit. She checked that she had scanning authorization so that she didn't get stuck with her foot in her mouth. Trying to scan a bleeding man without being able to check his file was a waste of time and possibly life.

George opened the door to the med bay for her, and she straightened her shoulders and walked inside.

Six men were on the med beds, and the first attending physician looked at her with a scowl. "Who are you?"

"Major Carter, Assessment Officer. May I be of assistance?"

The doctor frowned, but one of the men leaned up on one elbow, the other arm was missing. "It's Stitch!"

Suddenly, she had the attention of every conscious man in the room. She waved. "Hi."

Those that could waved back.

"We have a virgin in the back corner. Tell me what you would recommend." The doctor seemed to accept the recognition as her credentials.

Stitch headed to the corner where a man was lying and shaking with panic. "Hey, soldier. My name is Stitch, and I am going to be checking your options."

She stroked his forehead, and his eyes fluttered closed before they opened and pierced her with a panicked gaze. "Is it bad?"

"It isn't the worst I have seen." She

stroked his cheek softly.

She flicked open her scanner and ran the vid system down until she had seen all of the deep tissue scans that had been run on him.

She kept one hand on his face and ordered a nanite booster for him as well as several rounds of weaponry and high-stress legs that would enable him to move easily and leap twenty feet.

"I am going to check on the structure supplies and make sure that everything will work together."

He looked at her with wide eyes. "Don't leave me."

"I won't. I will do it all from here. I just have to stop touching you for a moment. You will still be able to see me."

He nodded. "Well, I guess I won't be a virgin much longer."

Stitch chuckled. "Nope. We all have to lose it sometime."

Everything she needed was in stock.

The doctor came over when she nodded, and she held out the order.

"Does he need that power pack?"

"To keep the legs functioning and using the boost option, yes."

He blinked. "You actually are *that* Stitch."

"Yes. Now, since he needs the nanite booster, you might want to get on that."

The physician grinned and left her alone. A med assistant came over with the booster and gave it to the young man who had lost both legs and one arm. The other was shattered. She stroked his cheek over and over until the sedatives took over. He didn't need to be alone right then.

Keenan Lukai was her focus until the team came to take him away.

She walked to the side of one of the cyborgs who had suffered a crushing injury. He patted the side of his bed, and she hopped up. "So, lazy. What are you in for?"

He laughed, and so did the man in the next bed.

Stitch spent the next few hours chatting with, flirting with and generally cheerfully tormenting all the men waiting to go into surgery or for replacement installation. When the damage warranted it, she upgraded their implants.

Finally, they were all out of the triage area and she could breathe.

George came in, and he smirked. "The ones out of surgery are requesting your attention, Stitch."

She nodded. "Right. Of course." She brushed at the front of her trousers, straightened her shirt.

This was what she did. She was the advocate for the wounded, trying to do what was best for them.

Keenan was still in surgery, but the others were out and getting their software upgrades.

There was a man in a bloodstained uniform speaking with one of the patients. Something was familiar about him.

She shrugged and went to check on the sergeant who was learning how to move his new hand.

"How is that going for you?"

He looked at it. "It feels different."

"It should. It has a blade extension that runs up the back of your wrist. It will come on line when you have mastered feeding yourself."

One of the other guys called out, "He will settle for being able to jerk off without ripping his dick off."

Stitch kept her expression bland. "It will be a good control test."

It was a little odd to see the men after

their implants were attached. The nanites were building seamless silver skin over the structures, and the men were rapidly becoming battle ready.

As she made the rounds to check on them, they all started to show signs of increased mobility. Feet flexed, hands flexed and their chests shuddered as their new organs kicked into play. The medical staff uncoupled them as the implants took their place in their bodies.

Stitch wondered what had taken place in her own system. Waking up with the implants functioning meant that they had had time to grow into her system. The hand felt like hers. It was even warm to the touch.

One of the men reached up with his silver right hand. She clasped it with her own.

His grin was one of pure joy. "It's a great fit."

"It is. I will send a letter of admiration to the manufacturer. Maybe I can get a long-distance thing going." She winked.

The other men laughed and jeered at the man still holding her hand. He flexed and pulled her toward him, so she responded with careful pressure.

His expression was shocked as she pulled him up and out of the bed. He was hanging from her grip, and the hoots from the other patients drew the angry eye of the medics.

"Major Carter, please put him down."

Stitch relaxed her arm, pulled away, and he settled back into the med bed.

"Why are you pestering the medic, Danforth?"

The voice was a new one. Stitch turned and looked at the brunette man wearing a skintight, sleeveless top and bloodstained black pants tucked into combat boots. The amazing thing was the colour that was riding the cybernetic arm. She had never seen designs on the silverwork before.

To her astonishment, the men in recovery snapped to a sort-of attention while lying down.

Danforth cleared his throat. "This isn't a medic, Captain. This is Stitch."

His features were sharp and reminded her of someone, but she couldn't quite place it.

The man walked right up to her and glared down at her with deep-brown eyes. She stared up at him, and he growled, "What will you give me if I go through with this?"

Recognition flared in her. "I will let you watch me eat a hot dog. Slowly."

He barked a laugh and hugged her. Stitch squeaked as he lifted her off her feet.

She patted the metal of his shoulders.

"Nice to see you again, Nikolai."

He looked at her and confusion came to his features. "Why are you here?"

"The explosion. All cyborgs must be shipped to the front lines as soon as they are mobile." She tapped him with her silver hand.

He set her carefully on her feet. "The base that blew? That was two years ago."

She smiled up at him. "Did all the beauty sleep work?"

Six men burst into applause. More hooting ensued.

He realized he was holding her, and he stepped back. "You look fine. Good. Lovely."

Danforth chuckled. "Maybe you should get your tongue replaced, Captain. You seem to have hit a stumbling block."

The others chuckled.

Nikolai glanced away from her, and

he was seeking someone. "Danforth, where is he?"

Stitch tapped his chest. "If you are talking about Keenan Lukai, he is in surgery, but let me check on it."

Nikolai was suddenly tense. "Is there a problem?"

"Let me find out."

She eased away from him and headed for the operating theatre. The door was sealed, but she was able to check the vid of the surgery. It was way outside of her paygrade, but she saw the surgeries and implants of the skeletal frameworks that would soon be his silver limbs.

The surgical team moved smoothly, and when Stitch had cut off the vid display, they came out with Keenan on the gurney, moving him to the recovery unit. The skeletal bases of his legs and his arm were visible, but the extra nanites were already moving through his system and grafting skin over the metalwork.

Three days and he would be up and running again.

She walked behind the gurney, and when she looked into Nikolai's eyes, she darted a quick look toward Keenan. Damn. Brothers. It was bad enough for one member of a family to be out on the front lines, let alone two.

"Nikolai, he needs to rest. His readings are stable, and the grafts have taken. He will be up and running soon."

She walked over and put her hand on Nikolai's arm, feeling the metal and tissue flex under her touch.

"I promised him I would look out for him."

"You did. He is alive."

Nikolai looked at his brother, lying still and silent under the sheet with the metal limbs extending. "Is alive enough?"

She patted him with her silver hand. "It is for me."

With nothing left to say, she turned and left him to stare at his brother. She had to order some mods to her own body so that she could move comfortably. With the men waiting for active implants, she would have to get in line, but it was better that she did it now. Who knew what tomorrow was going to bring?

Chapter Four

After she finished the paperwork for the parts she had ordered for the re- pairs on the men, her own requisitions needed the commanding officer's authorization.

She gathered the documents in her reader; she smiled at the use of the word *paperwork*. Paper hadn't been used for one hundred seventy-three years, and yet, it was still a reference for the tools of bureaucracy.

Stitch headed to the commanding officer's office and knocked on the door.

"Come in."

She stepped inside and was struck by the familiarity of the face that greeted her. "Nikolai?"

"Come in, Stitch."

She scowled. "How are you the base commander if you are a captain?"

"Scarcity. Alpha Base is on the front lines. When the satellites warn us, it is all hands to the ships. This place is a ghost town with the exception of the medical staff. They don't need an officer if there is no one to work on."

He waved for her to come in and sit. "Technically, you outrank me, so you can have command if you want it."

She scowled. "Give me a week."

He laughed.

She moved to the chair opposite the desk, and she sat. "I have the reports for the recent repairs and the new implants on your brother."

She opened her reader and flicked the report onto his desk.

He sighed. "I hate paperwork."

She laughed. "Right. Well, here is the requisition for some alterations to me."

When she flicked the information over, he stared at it. "What?"

"I need some ballast in my left arm; I have put in a requisition for reinforcement coils around my lower skeletal structure."

He frowned. "You want to go in again?"

"In?"

"To surgery."

"No, not particularly, but I wasn't assessing me when the parts were put in. The few ounces of unbalanced weight in my arms throw me off when I walk. The new organs have changed the structural integrity of my body, and my legs require reinforcement to compensate for the less efficient mineralization offered by the new organs."

He blinked. "So, what do you need?"

"You are the commander. You have to authorize my non-emergent alterations."

He looked down at the forms, including the outline of the female body with the marks on the necessary portions. "Is there anything else?"

"No. I mean, I wish I could run this past Cracker, but she isn't listed as being on active duty."

He chuckled. "Did you check your own status? You are still on medical leave. Cracker is awake, aware and designing new implants every week."

"Holy shit." Stitch leaned forward eagerly. "Can I contact her?"

He shook his head. "No, but you can send the request to her and see what she thinks. We will bounce it through a dozen satellites, and she will reply. A burst is the only way we can communicate with Omega Base."

Stitch nodded and pulled the file back

onto her screen, working quickly to send as much information as she could. She hummed quickly and sent the file back to Nikolai. "There. We will see what she can do with that."

He nodded and sent the file using a series of codes that she tried not to notice. Her analytical mind was already recording them before she thought to look away.

Nikolai smiled. "How long do you think she will need?"

"If she came through the explosion without brain damage? She will call back in three hours."

He nodded. "Would you like some lunch? It is time for a break."

"Sure." She got to her feet, and he got up and rounded his desk.

They walked in silence to the dining hall and didn't speak again until they were seated.

"So, Captain Lukai, how did you end up here?"

He smiled and forked up his meal. "Same way as everyone else. I went to the front line, and now, I am here. When the call comes, we go out, and if we are lucky, we come back."

"How did your brother get here?"

"He was a new assignment. They send them to us now and then. I had no idea he was coming. I tried to protect him, but he is a fighter and there was no stopping him." He shuddered. "Just as there was no stopping me."

"You survived."

"I wanted more from life than endless war. I wanted to return home a hero." He looked at her with his piercing gaze, and she was left speechless.

"You still can."

Surprise filled his gaze. "Didn't they tell you? They locked Earth against us.

There is no going home."

Her fork clattered to the table. "I thought they just put up shields."

"They did. They are safe as long as we keep the Splice from gaining momentum. That is our duty. We are the first line of defense, the barking dog on the outside of the perimeter."

"My family..."

He looked surprised. "You have children?"

"No. Parents, siblings. Can we send messages?"

Nikolai nodded. "We can. It is the same batch sending that we used to send the message to Omega Base."

She ran her hands through her hair. "Do they even know I am alive? Holy hells. This is..."

"Eat your lunch."

She couldn't eat. Couldn't think. She clutched at her head as her heart pounded. Her home. Gone. She had been kicked out, locked out, and no one had even bothered telling her.

Her mind sent her back to the moment where everything changed.

She saw the tag and read it; her mind went back to news vids of the last terrorist actions on Earth. The last three had all had a tag that read, From Your Secret Admirer.

Stitch heard herself yelling, and it was too late. Her mind recorded every moment of the bow being pulled, the flare of light, the glow of the explosion and then the wave of destruction as it spilled toward her.

She screamed as her friends were torn apart, and she was helpless to save them. The wave continued until it hit her and spun her backward. Her arm tore and shattered before she slammed into the wall. Her lower body went numb.

She heard Cracker calling for help, and she tried to crawl forward, but her arm wouldn't hold her.

"Stitch!" A hand was shaking her hard.

"Ow. What?"

She looked up at Nikolai, and he was standing next to her with concern on his face.

She was shaking violently, so she turned to her stone-cold food. The fork wouldn't hold her meal with her hand shaking, so fingers were put on food-acquisition duty.

Every face in the dining hall was turned toward her.

"What?"

"Stitch, you were screaming."

She nodded. "Probably. It was not a

nice memory to get stuck in."

She finished shovelling the cold food into her mouth and washed it down with a glass of water. At least the water was already cold.

She wiped her hands on her napkin and dabbed at her lips. Nikolai was still standing next to her.

"If you are waiting for me to blow you, I just ate."

He jerked slightly and tension left him. "Oh, good. You are still in there."

He sat across from her again. "That was disturbing. I have heard of others reliving their injuries, but I haven't seen it before. It was two years ago."

She smiled weakly. "It was the day before yesterday."

He smiled at her. "I will take a rain check on the blowjob."

"Good. How often does it rain here?"

Nikolai blinked rapidly. "Every few

weeks."

"Good to know." She winked and looked around the dining hall. "Is this everyone?"

"It is. When the base was first up and running, we had fifteen hundred men here. Now, we are down to one hundred and thirty-six, including support staff. We have more attack vessels here than we have pilots to fly them."

She smiled slightly. Her wish list to Cracker had included a control unit and software to fill up the storage inside it. She doubted that Nikolai had known the product codes or the software titles. If she was stuck on the front lines, she was not going to be helpless if the Splice came calling.

Stitch smiled. "Well, with lunch done, do you mind if I check on Keenan?"

He frowned. "You never checked on me after my surgery."

She tried not to smirk at his disappointed voice. "Sure I did; I just never entered the room. I had to check on my charges via their reports."

"I will come with you. He is my brother, after all."

She shrugged and got to her feet. "Come on, then, Base Commander."

He sighed and followed her.

The medics had Keenan on his feet. There was still a lot of tissue to grow in, and he was looking silvery but complete from hips to knees.

"Stop staring at his butt, Stitch," the dark murmur was whispered in her ear.

She smirked. "It is such a nice butt. How did you know?"

He stepped around her and headed for his brother. "I did some research on you after we met."

"You don't say. Were you looking into my preferences?"

Keenan looked at them and smiled. "If you two are here to visit me, you suck at it."

The medic grinned at them. "He is doing very well for his first."

Nikolai looked at his brother and scowled. "Why is he leaning?"

The medic looked wary. "It is a side effect of the surgery."

"I didn't have that."

Stitch stepped forward. "It is natural. He sees the difference in his limbs, and he moves to haul around a body with metal. His mind hasn't caught on to the nanites yet."

Nikolai frowned. "Why wasn't that an issue for me?"

She gestured to his hands. "You lost both and your lungs at the same time. You had more time to recover. A day makes a difference."

Keenan flexed his fingers and looked

at the tissue that was creeping up his new hand. "It is starting to feel like me again. Why is it silver?"

Stitch looked at the medic, and the medic gave her a nod.

"The nanites want to build the tissue and keep it functioning, but they can't graft to the metal work. They are programmed to build a bridge between the two structures. Basically, they are building metal skin and muscles as well as tendons. The connection in the jack point carries the nerve impulses from your new skin. You can feel like you did before, but you will have increased grip strength, faster reflexes with your fingers and your legs will be able to carry you for amazing distances without aching or breaking. If they are injured, a replacement can be plugged in in a matter of a few minutes, and your body will graft to it in a few hours. No more surgeries unless there are new, larger, injuries."

Keenan smiled. "Great. What is a jack point?"

She walked over to him and took his arm in her hands, feeling upward until the connector cuff was under her fingers. "The surgeons are needed to connect your existing body to the graft point, here. It has to have a solid foundation, and it is usually wired to additional spines that have been added to reinforce your body. Just because you have new limbs doesn't mean your original structure can handle what you can do with it."

"So, I can blast right out of my new skin?"

"Not your skin, but dislocated hips used to be a problem with the original structures. That is why I have a job. I have to check and double check that you are going to come out in one large, sturdy piece."

He grinned. "You are shorter than I thought."

Stitch smiled at him. "I made you two inches taller."

Nikolai growled. "Are you authorized to do that?"

She realized that she was still groping his brother's shoulder. "Touch your brother or make him taller? Either way, the answer is yes, I am authorized."

She patted Keenan and stepped away.

Nikolai put his hand on her shoulder. "Come on, soldier, you need a workout."

Stitch blinked and laughed. "Oh, please, let it involve getting naked."

He growled and shoved her out of his brother's vicinity. "Save something for the rain check, Stitch."

Chapter Five

Her arms trembled, she grunted and Nikolai's whisper encouraged her to push harder. Sweat made her grip slick, and she adjusted her grip on the column.

She pulled, and she made it to the top of the bar. "Fifty."

She dropped slowly and glared at him as she dangled from the bar. "You know that only one of my arms was replaced, right?"

He put his hands on her legs and nodded to her. "Drop."

Stitch slammed into his arms, and he caught her by the waist. Her breasts were even with his face. She saw his nostrils flare as he slowly lowered her down his body.

"Isn't this harassment or something?"

"Well, neither of us is fully human anymore, so do the rules still apply?" He held her against him, and he pulled her in flush with his body.

The workout gear she was wearing was no defense against the heat from his hands. His breath mixed with hers as she was slowly lowered to the floor. She smelled mint, and it made her smile before she wrapped her shaking arms around his neck. "I think that the rules can be bent a little."

She brushed her lips against his and whispered, "Just a little. I don't like things bending. I prefer them a little more rigid."

He smiled and brushed his lips against hers. "Perhaps another day. I just got confirmation that we have a burst from Omega Base."

She pushed against him and excitement burned in her. "Where? Where can I get it?"

"It has been sent to requisitions. I have to admit, I am really curious as to what all of that equipment is for."

"Don't worry. It will be made clear soon enough. Your guys have been limping along for a while. Haven't you noticed that the new cyborgs are less graceful than you are? It isn't because this is an outlier base; it was because you didn't have someone like me helping you out. I know all of the equipment, and now that I can communicate with Cracker, I can get all kinds of upgrades for the men installed in a matter of hours. The doctors do the work, but they don't look much beyond saving the patient. I can see the big picture."

He let her go, and the path they were

taking led to his office.

"If you don't see us as patients who need saving, what do you see us as?" He held his door open for her.

"Isn't it obvious? I see all of us as weapons. I try to make us as effective as possible." Stitch smiled brightly and sat in the spare chair in his office.

"Weapons?"

"Yes. We are. Even me, the doctors and the support staff that work on the base. All of us can be used as weapons. We just need to know how to pull the trigger."

"You are not here to be a weapon."

She cocked her head and wrinkled her nose. "Last night, I caught up to the news reports and what they are willing to give to us. No new staff. Only the frozen volunteers who were ejected from the Earth before they locked it. No communications in or out for civilians.

The weekly updates that you send are not answered. They want to forget about us, and if the Splice get past us, we will be a stain on human history. I want to make sure that doesn't happen, one warrior at a time."

He blinked. "You figured all that out last night?"

"Well, I was woken up by my own screams a few times, so I decided to do some research on what I have missed."

Nikolai leaned forward. "You are still having nightmares?"

"Memories. The last thing I remember. All those women lying in pieces, my friends bleeding and we were just having a birthday party. It took so much effort to get us all together, and there we were for the first time in months. They planned it so carefully for maximum damage. I am pretty sure I am angry. Very, very angry."

Understanding dawned on his face. "And it was all taken care of while you were sleeping."

"Sleeping, dead. Whatever. Apparently, I did my fair share of both." She shrugged. "So, I am all caught up, and I even have a good idea of the parts that are in stock as well as a list of replacements that are needed. If you authorize me to communicate with Cracker, I can put in an order and see what she can come up with."

"You know that your friend had a brain injury."

"It wasn't obvious, but I am not surprised. All of the survivors have had extreme damage, but there are only five more ladies who survived that party."

She flicked out her reader and glanced at him. "Why are we still listed as on medical leave?"

"The administration doesn't want any

live female cyborgs on record."

"What?"

"Yeah; they want us to pretend you don't exist."

"Why?"

"I wish I knew." He shrugged. "Nothing in the briefing bursts has stated why you are to remain camouflaged on the rosters."

"As long as I can find ways to contact the ladies from my station, I can live with being a hidden secret."

"So, do you want command of the base?"

The blunt question surprised her. "Ask me after the enhancements are in."

He leaned back in his chair. "How do you know so much about the enhancement program?"

"Ah. That. My parents were both scientists working with nanite programming, my brother was an alteration historian, and my sister was a micro me-chanic." The message from Cracker was listed between the lines of code that she had sent over.

Glad to hear you made it.
This should give you an extra boost.
Let's get this party started.

A slow smile spread across Stitch's lips. "You could say that I trained for this."

"Why did you volunteer?"

She looked at him and cocked her head. "Why did you?"

"To defend my world. I have parents, sisters and brothers, nieces and neph-ews. I wanted them safe."

"Same here. Well, no nieces or neph-ews that I know of, but my family is bril-liant, and I was the only one of us fit for duty. When the conscription tried to pass us over, I jumped in the truck."

She wanted nothing more than to communicate with her family, but she would need the code to send a secure message through the shielding. How fortunate that she was with the man who had the access to get her that code.

Sure, Cracker had sent it to her in thirty pieces, but getting the code out of Nikolai was going to be fun. She needed a distraction.

Nikolai growled. "So, you knew all about the implants."

"I did. I do. Only the theory though. I know how they interact with the human body and how the nanites bridge the gap as long as they have enough staff to do the job."

"If you aren't a scientist, how do you know all of this?"

"My family likes to talk. A lot. An extremely large amount. Some of it had to stick, and when the defense team took my family in to work on the first cyborgs, I went with them. I was like the Carter family mascot. I got coffee, tea and kept the reports flowing through the research department."

"And you picked it up as you went along." He nodded as if he had put it together.

"I did, and with every one of my guys that made it back into battle and stayed there, I got better at knowing what to put in the mix to keep them balanced and make them as whole as possible."

He chuckled. "Impressive. Who knew that the basic medical systems installed to keep humans youthful would result in something that could save their species? The vanity of humanity might just save us all."

She nodded. "There is one thing I haven't gotten access to."

"What is that?"

"Records of deployments. I have no idea how you actually fight the Splice."

He shivered a little. "That is part of our weapons system. You have to cut them and burn them out. Their bodies are caricatures of the species they have destroyed, and when you first see it, you get sick when you recognize human flesh. Men you have met and known are now embedded in monsters."

"Damn. Oh, Nikolai, I am so sorry." She had never thought of what happened to the dead fighters. It was something she didn't want to think about.

He nodded. "We get used to it, or we go mad."

"That isn't an option I want to think about." She wrinkled her nose.

"We have methods of working through things. Usually, we fight it out, but we keep others watching in case we go squirrely." He shrugged.

"I haven't ever seen a squirrel. Is there any wildlife here?"

"No, though there is an ancient city."

She sat up. "Seriously?"

"Yeah. We don't know how the atmosphere can be so compatible, but it was apparently the same thing as what was needed by the previous inhabitants."

"This isn't canned air?"

"No. We run it through a biological filter, but it is the same air that we have outside."

Her hands curled into fists, and she forced herself to relax them. "Can we go outside?"

The excitement in her system at the thought of being out on the surface of something that didn't have cables and monitors all over it was a wave of adrenalin she wasn't prepared for.

"I believe that you have an appointment with the medical staff. Based on their comments, they are excited. The coding that has come with the designs is ground breaking."

Stitch smiled. "It looks like Cracker isn't the only one awake." The coding was Lucky's strong point. It was a relief to know she had made it through. The head injury had been intense, and the visible damage was terrifying.

"I have to say, I have never heard of an administrative team with so many nicknames. That is usually left to the men of action."

She snorted. "That is sexist."

He shrugged. "It is true. So what's the deal?"

"It is sexist. Since the guys have nicknames, they have to take a step back when they can't just call us by our first names. It produces a barrier that removes sexuality from the equation."

Nikolai nodded as if it made sense. "So, where did Stitch come from?"

She made a face. "On my second week at Adaptation Base, I had a patient who came out of cold sleep, and he started crashing. His mind was trapped in the battle, and his body was missing a lot of parts. He needed a jolt to wake him up, so I climbed on a gurney and started using a stitch gun on his wounds. It was painful, but it was an action that his training accepted as a path to healing. He stabilized, and I was pulled off him as they went to put him in pre-assessment.

"I came back in later, and he didn't remember me, but he remembered someone cursing at him and giving him stitches. So, I became Stitch."

"You mentioned Cracker?"

"She had a repair on her table with a

malfunction. He kept grabbing her ass, so she grabbed a hammer and cracked his fingers open." Stitch grinned. "She then fixed him, but he stopped being grabby and spread the word."

"So, the names are a defense."

"One of many. We can all look up your files, and we know where your implants start and end. The right jab to the right pressure point and you are down for the count."

Nikolai smiled. "It is a good thing to remember, but I trust that no one on this base has made you feel uncomfortable."

She grinned. "Things are fine. What most men don't seem to understand is that it is a fine line between discomfort and fear. When that line is crossed, there isn't any going back. The woman either pulls back or attacks. We agreed to attack."

"Who is *we?*"

"The women of Adaptation Base. We had a meeting." She laughed.

A chime sounded from somewhere in his desk. "That is medical. They are eager to get started."

She nodded. "Right. I still want to know if I can go for a walk outside when this surgery is finished."

"We will see if we can find some exterior gear that fits you."

Stitch got to her feet and smiled. "I have a suit in my quarters. Just in case. Am I dismissed for my surgery?"

He nodded. "You are dismissed. I am curious to see what could possibly be so different about the coding your nanites have been given."

She grinned. "Lucky has a knack for putting the right code together. I am pretty confident about this."

One last look at Nikolai and she was

out the door, heading for the med lab where every doctor on the base was waiting to participate in her alterations. The funniest thing was the adaptations were all going to be administered by the automated surgeon. The doctors just wanted to watch.

It felt surreal to be giving the briefing while she stripped behind the privacy screen. "The adjustments that are going to be implanted today are to increase my quality of life and make the implants I have more effective."

"Why are you opting for the automated surgeon?"

She wrapped a thin cloth around her like a towel. "Because I have existing implants, the automation can work faster with the multitude of limbs it has. Keeping me splayed open for that long with a human surgeon would probably kill me."

"How will the automation minimize the problem if you are being opened all at once?"

"Shorter sedation period and my nanites can be set to numb my nerves. Now, if you want to watch, feel free, but don't interfere. The coding is very specific. Don't fuck with it."

She smiled brightly and climbed into the machine. Peeling away her wrap, she settled her tailbone against the calibration tab. The sharp stab of the sampler registered her identity, and the calibration began.

Bands held her limbs, and she was relieved that the machine knew that she had all parts intact.

She lost feeling in her limbs and the skin of her scalp, and the machines whirred to life. Sterilizing mist washed over her, and the blades and injectors came out. She could have closed her eyes, but she watched.

It would not be one of the moments that she sent home to her family if she was ever allowed to send a data packet home, but the details were needed to find out how the machines were behaving.

She couldn't watch as the upgrade port was added behind her ear. The drilling through her skull had her passing out from sheer self-preservation.

When she woke up, she was in the recovery centre, and there were flowers of several different varieties next to her bed. The doctors were deep in conversation, and her detailed stats were on the monitors all over the room. She was the only patient in the space.

She scooted up in the bed and stroked the flowers. "How long was I out?"

Captain Blue came to her side and checked her vitals. "Three days. The nanites kept you out, and the communication with Omega Base said it was completely normal."

She could see that he doubted it. A quick check below the sheet showed her what she had hoped. Each of her limbs now bore a silver line that indicated the reinforcement she had wanted. She tucked her sheet against her and raised her hands. Her arms were balanced.

"Do you feel any different?"

She grinned. "I feel balanced. Where is everybody? I thought that at least Nikolai would be here when I woke."

"He is off on a mission. There has been an incursion into our space, and the base is on minimal staffing."

Stitch sat up fully. "So, the entire base is evacuated?"

"No. All the fighters are gone. The medical staff and administration are all that is left."

Stitch flicked him a glance. "Can I get a wrap or something?"

"I have your uniform."

He turned and opened a cupboard next to her bed, bringing out her folded clothing and setting a pair of boots down on the floor next to the bed.

"We will leave you alone to change."

She snorted and flipped the sheet away. "Right. Like this whole area isn't crawling with cameras. I can see three of them from here."

She could see colour in his cheeks, but he turned his back anyway. She grabbed for the shirt with the shelf bra built in and adjusted her boobs when the knit fabric was on. Centuries of technology and they still couldn't make a brassiere in a shirt that didn't give her a uni-boob.

She slipped her feet into her panties and pulled them up over her new racing stripes. She felt a little tired, but by the time she was dressed and her hair was up in a bun, she was all business.

"Is there an ETA on the return of the troops?"

Captain Blue looked at her and did a double take. "No. Not currently. They will signal the amount of wounded and estimated injuries when they are on their way back."

She could feel that he was looking at her change of appearance and bearing. "Captain, am I clear for duty?"

"Uh, yes. All of your scans are good and your nanite communication is solid. While your physical capabilities are un-known, there is nothing to stop you from regaining your administrative duties."

She nodded. "Excellent. I will just get settled, and we will prepare to accept incoming wounded."

Blue frowned. "I beg your pardon?"

"I am now the highest-ranking command officer on the base, and I want the wounded treated in the proper order."

Blue gave her a shocked look. "We tend them in order of their chance of survival."

She nodded. "And that is a good thing, but you also want to make sure that while one major surgery is occurring, the auto-repair unit is in action."

He scowled. "The men don't like it."

"Then, it is a good thing I will be with them while the repairs are underway. I have familiarity with the unit. Not using it has crippled the base during the hours that could have had the majority of the survivors back on their feet."

"Are you saying that we shirked our duty? We have been here for years."

"And the number of cyborg virgins has dwindled. Save your skills for the full humans first and let the machines take care of the cyborgs."

She felt like an ass, but it was necessary. Having seen six men put ahead of Nikolai's brother because they were sharing surgeons was stupid and dangerous. If they had the repair unit, they should be using it.

Captain Blue scowled. "I am going to take this up with Captain Lukai."

"Feel free, in the meantime, have the labs and operating rooms prepped."

She turned and left him to take over the office. She had supplies to order and a communication link to take over. Just her average day at work.

Chapter Six

The alert came through, and Stitch took a look at the report. She set up the operation schedule and activated two dozen sleeper pods; it was all they had.

She grabbed her screen and headed to the medical bay. "We have incoming wounded."

Captain Blue looked up from the report he seemed absorbed by. "So? You are letting the machine handle it."

"Did you read what is coming in?" She growled at him.

One of the other doctors sneered. "The ship is on the way back. There were only a hundred cyborgs that were sent out. As you have stated, we can be replaced."

Stitch felt she should punch them one by one, but there wasn't time. "In fourteen minutes, a shuttle is landing with twenty men who have been taken apart by the Splice. We don't know their origins, but they are human, and you will get your asses in gear or I will rip off your arms and beat you to death with them!"

If Stitch was honest with herself, that last sentence was a little shrill, but the men did start moving.

Med bays were prepped, beds were readied and gurneys were rolled out. When the ship landed, they were ready.

Hours of shouting and confusion went by. Stitch hauled the cyborgs into the repair unit and talked to them the entire time they were being repaired.

Their upgrades were her little secret.

When Nikolai was lying in the unit, she smiled and croaked at him. "Well, you are a sight for sore eyes."

He smiled, and his crushed left arm twitched a little. "Are all my men taken care of?"

"Yes, and the wounded that you brought along are almost through surgery. How did you get your hand smashed?"

He wrinkled his nose. "I held up a door that wanted to come down. It came down anyway."

The machine whirred as it removed the damaged segments of his cyborg arm. To her fascination, as the replacement forearm and hand was plugged into place, his tattoo crawled down over the new skin as soon as it formed.

"That is neat."

"About a year ago, one of our maintenance techs found the code inside an upgrade for the repair machine. When activated with a four-digit code, it uploads a subroutine that caused the nanites to form designs."

"That code isn't five-eight-two-five, is it?"

He couldn't stare at her, but he chuckled. "Someone you know?"

"Lucky always bemoaned the lack of colour in the implants. I guess she got coding when she woke up." It made her giddy with relief that Lucky had been up for a year and had gotten straight to work. The possibility of brain injury had been high, so there was nearly tearful relaxation in Stitch's mind.

She now had a line on two of the survivors. The other three were still missing. Windy, Alphy and Lacey were still unaccounted for. They were still listed as alive but not officially on the books.

Stitch continued chatting with Nikolai until the machine opened, and he slowly sat up. Somehow, him being naked was a surprise, though she had helped the other men to their feet and clothing without a second glance.

She blindly groped for his clothing on the table beside her and handed it to him.

"I think that comes under the heading of sexual harassment, Stitch."

She jerked her gaze away from his crotch as he pulled on his pants. "Sorry. Oh, in case Captain Blue complains, I pulled a coup and have taken control of the base. Just thought you should have a head's up."

She looked at the machine and waited while he laced up his boots.

His placed his hands on her head, tilting her to meet his lips as he kissed her savagely to the point where he crowded her against the wall and lifted her until his pelvis was holding her in place.

She flushed hot, and the damp excitement between her thighs warned her that she was inches from ripping his clothing off. She pulled back.

He was grinning. "Thank you. I fucking hate paperwork."

Stitch fought for breath. "Perhaps you should put me down so I can get to the office and order replacements."

"Replacements?"

"Parts to replenish those used on the men that came in today."

The light of a thought came to his eyes. "Why weren't you with the men who had to go into surgery for the first time?"

"The cyborgs needed me more. Some of the guys freaked at having surgery done by a canister." She smiled. "There was a subroutine added to the implant design module. It came with the directions for my surgery, and it was implemented in every surgical data display and calculation as of two hours before you arrived."

"That was cutting it fine."

She shrugged. "It took me that long to find it. I was just sent a decryption key. The rest of the data arrived after I got all the new com codes and protocols."

He slowly eased back, letting her slide down the wall.

They left the surgery and headed for the recovery ward to see the new arrivals. The surgeons were still hard at work, but the newest cyborgs were all safe and monitored.

Stitch whispered to Nikolai, "I am on."

She sat next to the beds and touched shoulders and cheeks. Some of the men chatted with her as she explained what was going on. They had been captured eighteen months ago with an entire warship full of men. They were what was left. The Splice were using them up slowly.

One guy looked over with concern to the man in the bed next to him. "How is he?"

"He seems to have a high pulse, but he is recovering."

"Those guys, they fought hard every time the Splice came. They also all have weird marks on their back. I don't know what the Splice did, but it wasn't good."

"Excuse me."

Stitch went over to the man in the bed. He was still out, but his muscles were twitching.

She grunted as she rolled him to one side, and the long wounds on his back were already turning silver. The muscles were jumping in spasms.

She uncoupled him from the leads and pushed the bed toward the hall. "Nikolai, get the rest of them into cold units. They are going into shock."

Nikolai stared at her. "Why? Is there a problem?"

"Because they don't have the primer. They aren't human."

She could hear the other members of staff cursing as every mobile body grabbed a gurney and headed for the cold units.

"Stich, where are you headed?"

"The repair unit. I can use overrides to get a baseline calibration. The nanites need to be taught that these aren't humans."

She moved as fast as she could, skidding the gurney around the corner before shoving it through the doors of the surgery.

She really hoped that the adjustments

to her body had taken, because this was not the point to discover that she had failed. Stitch grabbed the man by the shoulders, and she lifted him. He grunted, but more of his muscles were twitching. She heaved and pushed, getting him into the module on her own. Stitch had to reach under him to find his tailbone, but the split bone simply confirmed that this wasn't a human.

She wracked her brain for the protocol for setting the machine up. The first thing she needed was an untainted tissue sample, so she took a plug from his shoulder and inserted it into the machine.

The calibration seemed to take forever, but when the lights went green, she took a deep breath.

Since it was habit by this point, she spoke to the man on the med bed. "This is going to be weird and uncomfortable, but it shouldn't hurt. As the first of your kind getting this treatment, we will be using you to try and save the rest of your men."

The machine chirped to announce that it was still ready, and she closed the lid.

"The first thing you will feel is the sterilizing spray. It will keep infection at bay. The next step will be a primer injection. It should take effect immediately, and your muscle tremors will cease. After that, the implants that were installed will take, and you will regrow your limbs to match your genome."

The injections were sliding into him, the blank nanites were reading his existing tissue and spreading the message to their buddies.

"There; you are being rebuilt from the bones out. The implants are grafted into your nervous system. It is amazing that the docs didn't see it."

To her surprise, the lifters came out and flipped him. The machines went into his back and started digging around.

Stitch watched as the machines removed plugs from the back of the man in front of her, and the marks immediately silvered over, becoming whole skin.

"So, the Splice put plugs in your back to keep something from growing back, maybe?"

The unit chirped completion, and the cover lifted. The hand that grabbed her throat was the metal implant that had been grafted on.

The man stared at her with rainbow eyes and a serious expression. He spoke harshly, and she choked. He shook her again, and her hair fell around her.

He must have been afraid of brunettes, because he dropped her to the floor. She got up and didn't back away from him.

"Hello. My name is Stitch, and I am currently in charge of this base. Now, I know you don't understand me, but we are also victims of the Splice."

He narrowed his eyes, and she felt a strange pressure in her head, like a headache was coming on.

He stood and looked at the raw metal struts that made up his arm. The flesh was growing down at a good rate, and astonishment came to his features.

"The skin will grow over it, and you will have a working hand. It will be silver, but it will be usable." She rubbed her neck lightly with her own silver hand.

He reached out and took it and held it next to his hand.

She smiled. "That is the idea." She flexed her hand, and then, she grabbed his neck and held him against the repair unit.

She gave him a serious expression as he choked. When his hand couldn't dislodge her, he surrendered, and she released him. She stepped back and crossed her arms, sure that he knew where she stood.

He bowed to her. It was a weird gesture to her, but she accepted it with a slight inclination of her head.

Stitch pushed past the gurney and got a set of clothing for him. She handed him the clothing, and he slipped it on. He got the pants on backward at first, but she didn't smile. She just waited until he figured it out and turned them around.

When he was dressed but barefoot, he cleared his throat. "Where are my men?"

She jumped at the English, but she explained, "We had to put them into cold storage while we worked on reprogramming you. Our doctors didn't realize you weren't our species, and the implants you were given were putting you into shock."

"It will become my hand again?"

"It will. Your feet are already covered."

He looked down and wiggled his toes as if noticing them for the first time.

"What were the plugs in your shoulders?"

Excitement came to his eyes. "You removed them?"

"Yes."

"Our wings grow back." His smile was slow.

"Well, that is something. Come on, help me get this gurney back to the pre-surgical area, and we can begin bringing your men in."

"How many of us were rescued?"

"Fifteen, including you. The rest were our men."

"Can I see them?"

"Yes. They are in cold canisters, so we have to take them out one at a time. I think most of them have been repaired and enhanced, but the canisters will slow the acceptance of the implants; it will also keep them from dying because the nanites don't know what to do."

"I don't understand."

"I will tell you later. Come with me."

She led him to the pre-op area, where the canisters were humming. Nikolai was helping get the last of the quivering aliens into the cold canister.

"Stitch, did it work?"

"Ask him yourself. He understands English now."

Nikolai looked from her to the stranger, and his eyes narrowed. Stitch didn't know he could move that fast, but he grabbed the man and held him in the air. "You touched her!"

Veins were standing out in Nikolai's neck, and he looked like he was going to break the stranger's head against the wall.

"Nikolai, stop it! Put him down. I already strangled him!"

He looked at her in surprise and let the alien go. The man landed on his feet with a weird grace.

The medics were standing around and staring at the stranger with confusion.

She checked the canisters until she found the most likely candidate for an easy transition. The more the automated repair unit could learn, the faster the corrections would be.

All of Lucky's and Cracker's lectures were finally hitting home. She never thought that it would come in handy to have all this crap in her head.

"This is the one who goes next. Can someone give me a hand getting him onto a gurney?"

"Stitch, is it a good idea to increase the amount of an alien force on our base?" Nikolai was scowling.

"I think it is stupid not to help men so close to our own that the surgeons couldn't tell them apart." She keyed in the access code and warmed up the man who began to shake immediately.

The stranger stepped forward. "I will carry him."

Nikolai shook his head. "No, you shouldn't put weight on your implant. I will do it."

Technically, Stitch could do it, but she wasn't a fan of heavy lifting.

Nikolai picked up the twitching alien, and Stitch led the way back to the machine. When the cold, naked man was laid in the unit, she used her hand under his ass to line him up with the machine.

His arms and legs were minimally damaged, but she had to set the machine with a skin sample just as she had with the first stranger.

When the lights indicated it was go time, she stayed next to the machine as it whirred to life.

She told him what was going to happen, and when the stranger came toward the machine, she held Nikolai back as he began to speak in the whispery language that had sounded so hoarse when he shouted it.

He tensed when he saw the needles with their silver contents, but she explained nanites as best she could.

When he paused, she continued to explain as the machine rotated the new patient and what it was going to do to the wounds in his back.

The stranger whispered to his friend, and Stitch got the mental image of flying.

When the machine chirped its completion, Stitch opened the unit and let the stranger catch his buddy when he came out.

The men hugged and stood close together.

Nikolai pulled Stitch aside. "Are you sure that this is right?"

"They were being carved up by the Splice. That is enough credential for me."

He looked back, and the two strangers were looking at them.

The first one smiled. "I am Commander Liakon, this is Sergeant Aluak. We are at your service in fighting the Splice. As are the rest of my men."

Stitch winced. "Damn, I am going to have to find quarters for them."

Nikolai smirked. "The joys of being in charge."

Stitch poked him in the chest. "Go and get another one so we can get them into their own beds. And find some pants for that guy."

Nikolai nodded and saluted. She turned around and stalked back to the sleeper canisters and lined them up in order of priority.

She had one of the medics carry the next patient into the machine and showed him how to line the guy up and take the sample.

When everything was ready, the door closed and Liakon and Aluak were watching closely.

"Why do you take the sample?"

"To tell the machine you aren't human. It changes the program and lets it do things like analyze what your bodies should look like and then build them again."

"And those shots?"

"They provide a bridge between the programmed bots that are causing the problem and the implants, including organs."

"You can replace organs?"

"Everything but the brain, and even that has some wiggle room."

The medic looked at her nervously. "Major Carter, you are going to leave me here?"

"Unless you have authorization to accept five human and fifteen strangers to the base and find quarters for them all, yeah, you are up."

She smirked. "Nikolai, when you are done finding a stack of clothing for them, feel free to help carry the men in for treatment. You are best suited for heavy lifting."

He stuck his tongue out at her, and

she laughed as the door closed between them.

<h1 style="text-align:center">Chapter Seven</h1>

She sent a note on the aliens to head-quarters with a mention of how she was keeping them under surveillance, whatever that would entail.

With that taken care of, she ran through the usage of implants and equipment, putting through requisitions for the parts that couldn't be manufac-tured with the machines on base.

Her stomach growled and alerted her to the passage of time. Stitch finished the essentials and got to her feet, stretching before the long walk to the dining hall.

The few men that she met in the halls nodded politely and addressed her as major.

She patted the loose bun that she had managed to wrangle her hair into and smiled. It seemed that the trick still worked. Girls with their hair down were free to flirt with; hair up meant business.

Her bones were tired when she went to the machine and got a pre-packaged ration to eat. The hot breakfast wasn't starting for hours.

She dragged herself to a table and prodded at the meal with her fork. It had been one exceptionally busy day, and there was so much more to do.

"Stitch. Stitch. Wake up." Nikolai's voice whispered in her ear.

She cracked her eyes open and saw his concerned face inches from her own. "What?"

"The new arrivals wanted to speak with you, so we went looking."

She sat up and looked past him where fifteen men were lined up, each with military bearing and all staring at her.

Her food was cold. She must have been out for several minutes at least.

She looked around and saw the clock. "Well, hell. I have now gotten to the point where I can sleep sitting up. Evolution at work."

She smiled at Nikolai and said, "Have them pull up some tables and chairs. Standing up is not really an option."

The men obviously heard her. They pulled in tables and surrounded her in a semi-circle.

Nikolai stood behind her. She could feel the heat coming off his body.

Commander Liakon cleared his throat. "Major Carter, we are thankful that you have accepted us as guests at your base."

Aluak inclined his head. "Your timely

assistance saved our lives."

Liakon cocked his head, his rainbow eyes staring at her. "How did you know?"

She answered honestly. "My family assisted in designing the programming, and if a person had not received the initial introduction of the nanites before the implant was attached, the seizures would begin. The active repair nanites would start tearing the body apart, but not know how to put it back together. They are machines, but we have to tell them exactly what to do."

Liakon nodded. "How do we remove them?"

"You don't. They are part of you now. For some of you, they are running the organs implanted; for others, they maintain the balance of skin and bone. Yours are now part of you just as mine are part of me."

He frowned. "It can't fall into the hands of the Splice."

She nodded. "That is true, but it won't. Our men who have fallen into the hands of the Splice, including those who were retrieved with you, have already had the nanites and live with them. They had them before they went to battle, and they have them now."

Aluak scowled. "If the Splice have this technology, why aren't they using it?"

"The nanites are programmed for the possibility that they will be separated from their host. Without a working immune system, they burn out."

The men looked sceptical, so she took her knife and cut her normal hand. The men gasped, and she dripped a puddle of blood on the table.

It bubbled and scorched until there was nothing but ash.

"Severed tissue does the same." She

held up her hand so they could see that the cut was healing at an accelerated rate.

Stitch smiled. "I am not recommending that you all try, but now, your bodies can recover rapidly from any damage inflicted with the exception of having a limb or organ destroyed. Those need frameworks to build tissue around."

Liakon nodded as if it made sense. A slow smile crossed his features. "Do you have a lover, Major Carter?"

She was about to open her mouth and speak when Nikolai said, "Yes."

She shrugged with a smile.

Liakon nodded in agreement. "If you ever have need of one, please consider me or one of my men for the position. We all have extensive training in the arts of love, and it would be an honour to be at your service."

"Um, thank you. I will keep it in mind

if there is an availability. I do have a question for you and your men."

"Please, do not hesitate."

"The question is twofold. The first part is what are your kind called, and the second is do you have anyone who can make a scale drawing of your wings, including tensile strength and lift capacity? We may be able to speed the regeneration if we can install frameworks that will help your body repair."

"Solouk is a biologist. He should be able to reproduce what we have lost."

"How long does it normally take for your wings to regrow?"

"Six months."

She made a face. "How long were you a prisoner?"

"Our ship was captured a week ago. Your men were already on board. It was a shock to see the men coming to rescue their own, and we were even more astonished when they took us with them. We were grateful; we are grateful, but for one species to take in another in the face of war is amazing."

Nikolai sighed. "To be honest, we didn't know you weren't ours. You look the same."

Stitch was surprised. "You didn't notice their eyes?"

Liakon cleared his throat. "We did not let them see. The Alguth are sensitive when it comes to the minds of other species. When we saw how close we were to your kind, we blended in."

"So, a chance to escape was in front of you, and you took it?" Stitch fought her smile.

"Yes."

"Well, I am delighted that you have all made it out alive. Now, did Nikolai show you where you are staying?"

The world was getting warm and

blurry again. She listed to one side before she jerked upright.

"Stitch, we should get you to bed."

She chuckled. "It is nearly dawn. I will have to be up in two hours to check the communications."

"I will help."

She swayed again, and he sighed. "Executive decision."

She figured out what it meant when he lifted her and carried her out of the dining hall with fifteen aliens walking behind them. To her surprise, he didn't take her to her quarters; he brought her to the med lab and put her in the machine.

"We use this before we go on a mission. It helps keep us awake without doing any damage."

She wrinkled her nose. "Recalibrate it for me."

He laughed. "I know how to set it."

She lay back and watched the machine as it whirred, but instead of needles and scalpels, she saw light. Her mind relaxed and her body went boneless for a moment.

Her skin was tingling when the machine opened again. She felt bright, refreshed and ready to tackle the day.

Nikolai smiled when she swung her legs out of the machine. He put his hands on her waist. "Better?"

She pulled his head down and kissed him with a portion of the energy ripping through her.

His hands contracted on her waist, and he pulled her in close. She wrapped her thighs around him, and he cupped her buttocks as they ravished each other, tongues sliding and hearts pounding.

He moved his hand up her spine, and she shivered. When he gripped the back of her head, her hair came loose again and he groaned.

She pulled away and smiled at him. "So, you want to help me work off this energy?"

"In front of your guests?"

She looked past him to the group of aliens who were watching with amused fascination.

Stitch didn't even think before she said, "That wouldn't bother me, but this lab isn't really comfortable. Perhaps something a little more horizontal?"

Liakon smiled. "We will explore the exercise facility and determine what we can do with our new limbs."

Stitch frowned. "Take it easy. It will take a few more hours until the integration is complete."

"Yes, Major. We will follow your dictates."

She looked at Nikolai as the aliens filed out. "You could take a lesson from them."

He started to walk with her still wrapped around him. She smirked at him the whole way.

When they were inside her quarters, he whispered in her ear and said, "I will fulfill all your requests and try to entice you into a few demands you didn't even know you wanted."

"Fine, remove my uniform."

The moment he knelt in front of her, she knew they were off to an excellent start.

Chapter Eight

Her throaty order for him to remove his own clothing was lost in the rustling and occasional tearing of fabric. It wasn't until he leaned down and unlaced his boots that she had time to focus on what was going on. Naked and settled on one side while she looked at him, she focused on why he was there at all.

If he had imprinted on her because she kept him sane in those moments before his surgery, she was going to be braced for his eventual coming to his senses. Her heart would break, but in the meantime, she could fill it with memories. When they got back to Earth, if they got back to Earth, they would go their separate ways. She was pretty sure that Nikolai could do better than a damaged organizational freak.

"What are you thinking about? It can't be good."

He was taking off his pants and skimming out of his underwear in one move. His skin was dotted with silver patches that indicated internal reinforcement, but it didn't deter from his beauty.

The nanites had been designed for folks who wanted the vanity of physical alteration without the worry of rejecting the implants. It was a fad that had led to their ability to defend themselves a century later.

"I was thinking about how we ended up here."

He stalked toward her. "That is a very heavy subject, Stitch. I think you need a distraction."

She watched his approach, and she smiled. "I think you are right. I won't say that often."

He crawled over her and lowered his lips to hers. "Mission *Distract Stitch* is commencing."

She smiled against his mouth. "Thanks for the warning."

The kiss started out soft and grew deeper and more savage with every passing second. She turned her hips to invite his thighs to move between hers.

The smooth feel of his hands on her skin spurred her analytical side, but when he broke their kiss and cupped her breasts, the analysis of the texture of his adjustment disappeared.

She sighed as he sucked at her breast and tugged her nipple between his teeth. She could feel her folds getting wet with each tensing pull on her skin.

Stitch gripped his shoulders then cupped his head, directing him from one breast to the other.

She squirmed against him and wished his hair were longer. As it was, she had to use her strength to put his head where she wanted it. A low chuckle let her know that he didn't mind.

When he started working lower, she squeaked and tried to pull him up, but the sneaky bugger held her hands down and crept backward, kissing and sucking his way between her thighs.

He tongued her folds apart and lapped at her. The flat expanse of his tongue delved into her, drinking her as her body put out its slick invitation.

She clenched her fingers around his as he held her to the bed. The top of his head was moving in time to his tongu-ing, and when she screeched, he re-leased her hands, pulled up and fitted his cock to her, working inside as her muscles clenched and drew him inside.

He shuddered, and sweat broke out on his skin.

Stitch wrapped her hand around the back of his neck and pulled him toward her as he started a slow thrust that undulated him against her.

Nikolai caressed her tongue with his as he rocked into her with a steady beat.

Stitch moved her hands down his body, dragging her fingers down his sides and finding where metal and man became one. She bit at his lips as they kissed and stroked the deep groove in his spine, coaxing him into a faster beat.

She pulled at him and hooked her right leg around him.

He broke the kiss and lifted up, staying inside her as he pushed her legs back until her knees were nearly to her chest.

He slid in deeper, and the breath left

her lungs. She wanted to call him a cheater, but instead, she moaned.

He thrust into her with fervent determination. His teeth were clenched, and the veins on his neck were distended as he fought for control.

She reached between them and took her new hand for a spin, moving in rapid circles around her clit until she was caught in a whirlwind of bright sparks behind her eyes.

Nikolai grunted hoarsely and let out a low growl as he spilled into her. He jerked his hips sharply against her, and he finally stopped holding her legs in the tucked position.

After he pulled out, he dropped to the bed beside her. "Well, I can cross that off my list."

She nodded. "Me too."

He put his hand on her stomach. "I didn't mean it to sound like that. It has just been a fantasy of mine for a very long time."

Stitch looked at him, and there was a very concerned expression on his face.

She nodded. "I am sure that after my face gets put on one of the sex bots in the rec centre, you will get over it."

"Do you think that this is just a lark for me?" He scowled.

"No, but I am also cognizant of the fact that I am the only woman on this base and that guys race to see who can get in the lady's pants first."

"This isn't like that. None of the other guys would dare get into your bed. They don't think of you like that."

She snorted. "Great to know."

He sighed and pressed his forehead to hers. "I am making a hash of it."

"A little bit."

He sighed.

She took pity on him and turned toward him, facing him.

"Let's start again, Nikolai. Neither of us was at our best when we met."

He sighed. "Call me Nik or Niko."

"Call me Stitch." She reached toward him and took his left hand with her right. "I am a recent cyborg and OCD administrator. There isn't a military bone in my body... well, not since you pulled out."

He quivered with laughter. "I have been a cyborg for three years, in charge of the base for eighteen months and have hated the paperwork the whole time."

"I started working in assessment back on Earth and volunteered to come out to help the war effort even after I knew it would mean mandatory sterilization."

His fingers squeezed hers. "I had nightmares when my brother told me he was enlisting."

She smiled sadly. "I cried when I had to work with my first wounded fighter, but I waited until he was headed to surgery before I let go."

"I was scared stiff when I was thawed out for enhancement until an angel walked me through the procedure and promised to let me watch her eat a hot dog if I survived. I never did get to collect on that."

She chuckled. "Your eyes were so pretty. Still are actually. It hurt to go through assessment and the team manipulation, never seeing the men again. Being here has been nice when I see some of my men again."

"Am I included in the wounded assessment?"

He squeezed her hand.

"Every inch of that initial repair to you was my design. I chose the pieces one by one that would make you better able to survive the next fight. It looks like I did a good job, but I never thought of any of the guys as wounded, not after the first. You were all just on your way to be stronger. It was a fiction I maintained until I had time on my own."

"How many?"

She knew what he was asking. "One thousand nine hundred and thirty-four, including your brother."

He quirked his lips. "So, you have done me and my brother. That may cause issues."

She snorted and squeezed his hand again. "Funny."

He grinned.

"Who did you leave behind?"

He sobered. "My parents and I thought I had left Keenan behind. He proved me wrong."

She chuckled. "He is alive, and if the Earth will let us come home when this is over, he has a chance at a family."

"You don't?"

"Well, they froze my ovaries, but it isn't like they can be put back in. The nanites would seek out any genetic intruders and destroy them. My sister said she would try and have a daughter for me if I came back."

He frowned. "I didn't know that. I thought that they altered the programming to allow for children. That is what we were taught."

She sighed and held up her silvered hand. "The would-be mothers don't have to support an artificial skeletal structure. The introduction of the implants changes the entire situation."

"So, they removed your ovaries."

"Yup, and put them into cold storage."

He smiled. "Well, they sterilized us before we left, after taking a working sample, so I hope that one day my popsicles can meet your popsicles."

She laughed. "If my sister gets pregnant, it would be the weirdest three-way ever."

He grinned and leaned toward her for a short kiss. "She means nothing to me."

"Her husband will be delighted to hear it."

She sighed and ran her hand down his chest. The silver skin had better senses than her other hand. Her left hand only felt the strength and heat of him and was currently wedged under her so had no opinion of his body's texture.

"I was afraid that you wouldn't want to touch me." His confession came out against her lips.

"And I was worried that you would get nervous when I did this." She trailed a hand down his chest, over the cobblestone abs, and she gripped his cock.

He tensed. "Oh. That."

She stroked her fingers under his shaft and caressed his balls while he shivered. She kept her touch gentle, but he groaned when she finished cupping his balls and wrapped her fingers around his shaft.

"You see, there aren't a lot of men on this base who would let me take my cybernetic hand and wrap it around his cock, let alone do this."

She massaged him, tugging carefully as his erection grew again under her touch.

"I have always had less of a self-preservation instinct than I should have." His eyes closed. "It has always worked out for the best."

She laughed and continued to stroke him as she squirmed around until her lips were inches from the angry head of his cock.

Stitch took him into her mouth and sucked on him, pulling back and then moving forward, breathing in through her nose on the stroke toward him.

He muttered, and she felt his hands in her hair. She continued sucking at him until his fingers started to tighten. The moment he pushed down on her head, she pulled away and replaced her mouth with her hand.

There was some resistance to her backing away, but she pulled away with insistence.

She kept jerking him off while she shifted until they were face to face again. "The next time you are in the commissary, jam a whole cucumber down your throat, and then, we can discuss pushing my head down on your dick."

He blushed and then grunted as he came. The cum struck her belly, and she sighed. Time for a shower.

Stitch patted his shoulder. "I am heading for a shower. You are welcome to join me."

He looked at her with dazed eyes. "I think that would be a good idea."

She crawled over him and dropped to the floor before straightening and walking to the bathroom. She fired up the shower and stepped under the hot spray, washing away the cum and easing the ache between her thighs. She was out of practice even before her two-year cold sleep.

He slipped in behind her and got his hands into the shampoo dispenser, lathering up her hair before she could even turn around. The scalp massage was worth any previous gaffes. He definitely had a skill when it came to rubbing her scalp.

"What is this?" He paused as his fingers pressed the new jack she had requested.

"Oh, that is my booster kit. If I ever have to go out in the field, I want to be able to fight, so it is an education jack that lets me learn combat very quickly. Or surgery or medical treatment. I already got the med library. I am just letting it settle."

She turned and faced him; the water slowly rinsed her hair. With the flick of a lever, she started up the second showerhead, and he was pelted from behind.

"Wow. You got the fancy shower."

"It matches mine on the old base. I wonder how it is doing?"

He wiggled to get the heat on his back and groaned. "It is still in operation, but it has been attacked twice by the Splice."

"What do the Splice look for when they attack? How does the fighting go?"

"They come at us in a rush of stunners and blades. They cut us to bleed us, and their numbers are such that they drag off our wounded before we can stop them."

She soaped her breasts and then between her thighs while he watched. "And is there a log or record of the attacks that I can see?"

"We archive all of the footage. Our battle suits all have a link to the battleship we arrive on, and it uploads to the base when we arrive."

"What happens to the recording if they are captured?"

"The units are usually destroyed as soon as they are removed. Our men are kept naked to avoid hidden weapons."

"Do they have a language?" She finished lathering between her thighs, and she turned to wash away the soap.

"They do, but we can't understand it."

He scrubbed her back and kissed her

shoulder. "You shouldn't think about it."

"I have to. There has to be a way to end this. We have been at it for twelve years, and Earth is dumb enough to think that they can survive behind that shield. One crack in it and they are toast."

He chuckled and paid attention to his own shower while she finished her scrubbing and headed out.

The wrap absorbed a lot of water, and when her hair was towelled dry, Stitch returned to her room to get dressed.

She had attack patterns to look into and an alien race to learn about. At least Niko hadn't fought her for power.

She needed all the support she could get.

$$\text{Chapter Nine}$$

After a long, late night and early morning of looking at horrific battle vids, she understood a little more about the Splice. What she understood was that their ships' systems were linked, and they could find out a lot about the Splice if they could just get into their computers.

Stitch needed a workout. The adjustments that she had installed needed to be tested.

She headed off to the gym and saw the aliens working out, in awe of their new body parts. George was wandering around and helping them with the equipment. It seemed that some of the military were all right with the newcomers.

She found an empty machine, strapped weights to her legs and started doing pullups.

When she finished with the pullups, she went to the bench press and dialled up what she figured she could move comfortably.

The two hundred pounds was too easy, so she went to the controls and turned the weight up to two-fifty then three hundred, three-fifty, and no matter what she was lifting, she could always lift more.

"Fuck." She got out of the machine and went to the pressure station. She put her hands and feet in the slots, lowering the plate to her height to gradually take the weight.

"George, can you give me a reading?"

"Sure thing, Stitch." He left the man

he had been talking to and wandered over to watch as the pressure built on her hands and body.

She pressed upward and triggered the machine. The wide plate above her began to bear down on her, so she simply had to push back.

"Four hundred, four-fifty, five, five-fifty, six, six-fifty, seven, seven-fifty... close, so close. Come on, Stitch. You can do it."

Her mind was going a little blind with the effort to keep the plate up. She gave one final shove and dropped to the floor. The plate dropped down a few inches before it stopped itself.

"Congratulations, Stitch. You pushed eight hundred kilos."

She looked at him in horror. "I thought it was set to pounds."

He looked at the machine and grinned. "Nope. Eight hundred kilos.

You can lift a small vehicle if you need to."

He gave her a sly smile. "What about the strike plates? Have you tried them?"

Stitch crawled out of the pressure unit and stared at him. "You just want to watch, don't you?"

George shrugged. "Since you and Nikolai have focused on each other, watching you in action is the next best thing."

He helped her to her feet, and she wrinkled her nose at him. "Pervert."

"You have no idea. Okay, the strike plate."

The Alguth warriors were watching her, and when she cleared the pressure machine, they started taking turns.

Apparently, knowing how much you could lift was a very important thing to the Alguth.

She wrapped her knuckles and faced the strike plate. Thick gel was filled with sensors packed behind a skin-like structure, and the wires were designed to see how hard a cyborg or human could punch.

"The machine is ready. Any time, Stitch."

She glanced over her shoulder, feeling Niko come in. The other cyborgs wandered in, all with their workout gear on. She made a fist and plowed her natural hand into the plate.

George nodded. "Seventy-three kilonewtons. Excellent. Now try your natural hand." He had slight condescension in his tone.

"That was my natural hand." She hit the reset with her knuckles and got ready. "This is my cyborg hand."

She slammed her hand forward, and the rig shuddered.

The display blanked, and it slowly displayed the impact force if she put herself behind it.

"Stitch, I am tempted to hack off my hand if that is the result."

She looked at the force recording and grinned. She couldn't help it. The number six-six-six was displayed in bright numbers.

Captain Blue came by and stared from the readout to her. "That should have shattered every bone in your body."

She smirked. "Probably. That is why I had the extra surgery."

Niko came up behind her and looked at the readout. He whispered in her ear. "You handled my cock with that?"

She chuckled and turned until she was nearly kissing him. "Quit whining. It is still attached, isn't it?"

He kissed her quickly, and she smacked him on his butt. "Let's see what you can do."

"Somehow, this is not the venue I

thought you would say that in.”

She watched George recalibrate the machine, and Niko took his shot. After him, Keenan wanted to try, but though Niko scored at one hundred fifty kilonewtons, no one else even managed to get close.

Liakon came over and sat next to her on the bench. “Major Carter, how did you do that?”

She smiled. “I designed myself.”

“I beg your pardon?”

“I told the engineers and programmers what I wanted my body to do, and they provided me with what I needed.”

“Can we do that?”

She shook her head. “No, you can probably punch at twice your species’ norms, but I only experimented on myself.”

“So, what you did was dangerous.”

“It could have been, but I am committed to my situation as a cyborg and no longer a proper member of my species. So, I decided to be the best cyborg I could be."

She unwrapped her hand as she felt the skin had recovered. "So, tell me about the Alguth."

He watched her examine her hand, but he spoke.

"My world contained approximately two billion people. We had a very small standing military and were just at the point where peace had reigned for five decades when the Splice attacked."

"Did you have any kind of space fleet?"

"No. We waged a ground defense. The cities were able to erect shields, but it has confined its citizens. For us, being caged is akin to being crippled."

It was a hard question, but she had to ask. "How many of your people survive?"

"Less than half. A quarter of the populations encased succumbed to depression." He looked grim.

"So, how did you learn my language, because it is *my* language you shared with the rest of the guys."

"Our kind are adaptable. It is the reason that our people were hunted by the Splice. They want our camouflage and are trying to figure out how to get it."

She chuckled grimly. "They want the human ability to store fat, as well as the grafting options available with our skin. When did they attack?"

"Five solar cycles ago. How long for you?"

"Twelve years. Our world is also sealed now."

"How do you get supplies?"

She chuckled. "We ask very nicely."

"Can Solouk draw the pattern later?"

"Sure. It will take a few hours to learn what we need to make it happen. It will mean that you have to go back into the machine again."

"That is fine. I will be the first to go through it. None of my men will undergo the experiment until I have gained a set of working wings."

"Right." She unwrapped her metal hand and flexed her fist. "Well. I will get back into office and Solouk can meet me after he finishes playing with the strike plate."

She tossed the wraps in the cleaner and headed to her office, positive that there was a lot of paperwork waiting for her.

As she sat and looked through the communications that had come in, she had to admit her instincts were on point.

She had never seen screaming in a

communication before, but Earth Control was highly irritated with her taking over Alpha Base.

She replied to him that if he wanted to come out and take her place, he was welcome to it.

The grin on her face when she filed the note in the outgoing batch was pure evil.

Solouk was sitting in a corner of her office and drawing on a tablet, working on the dimensions and tensile strength of the wings.

She brought up the weight of the heaviest of the Alguth and asked, "How many of your own people can you carry with those wings?"

"Just ourselves."

"Do you want to carry more?"

He looked up, "How much more?"

"One of your men?"

He smiled slowly. "That would be

amazing. Our wings have simply been a means of transport."

She nodded and set up the spec sheet for the alterations. "How is the schematic coming?"

"I feel it is pretty accurate."

She extended her hand and beckoned to him. "Hand it over."

He got to his feet, and she took the tablet, looking at the wide dragonfly-style design and the data included as to dimensions and structure.

"Good. Let's see what the mechanic and the programmer do with this."

She wrapped it up and sent it through the data burst with a note for Windy.

"Now we wait." She smiled. "Feel free to run off with your men and see who can out-punch me."

"I would like to ask you a few questions."

"Certainly."

He cocked his head and smiled slowly. "Do you think you will tire of Captain Nikolai?"

She blinked in surprise. "Um, I hadn't given it much thought. I might, or he might tire of me."

"Commander Liakon would be an excellent choice for you, Queen Stitch."

She held up a hand. "What did you call me?"

"For the Alguth, a woman in your situation is a hive queen." He smiled encouragingly. "It is important for you to have a mate that matches your power."

"I am fine with Nikolai. I will make sure to keep you posted."

"If you insist. They will fight it out eventually, I am sure."

She was left confused and stunned as Solouk left her with a concern she hadn't imagined before. Aliens at the gate and they wanted in her underwear.

Chapter Ten

Four hours of answering data missives and getting replies to the requisitions later, she realized she was hungry.

Stitch headed to the dining hall, and she rubbed the back of her neck as she walked. It was nice to be on her feet again, but the back tension of the office chair was tremendous.

After lunch, she was going to go exploring. She wanted to get into her bio suit and see what there was to see.

The dining hall was in full swing, so when Stitch had her meal, it took her a while to find a spot to sit down.

Niko was sitting with the Alguth, and he got to his feet as she approached.

There was one seat across from him, and she slid into place with a sigh.

She winked at him. "Wake me if I fall asleep before I eat again."

The Alguth chuckled and welcomed her to their table.

She nodded her thanks and attacked her meal.

Five minutes of silence ruled over the table, and when she finished her cutlet, potatoes and vegetables with the fruit cup she had slammed down like a shot of whisky, the men at the table were looking at her warily.

"Apologies for the hurry, but I only have a few more hours before the data burst comes in, and it might contain those designs I am waiting for."

Niko bracketed her legs with his. "What are you going to do for a few hours?"

"Put on my suit and head outside. I

want to get a feel for where we are."

Niko frowned. "Are you sure you should be doing that? You are in charge of the base."

She grimaced. "Consider it my time off, Mom."

He blinked, and a slow smirk crossed his features. "That is something I have never been called."

She grinned. "I have an entire arsenal of names for you. I plan to bring them out one at a time."

The Alguth men smiled. Apparently, this didn't alarm them.

She looked at the empty tray, sighed and got to her feet. "Well, gentlemen. I will see you later."

Liakon rose. "Do you need someone to accompany you?"

Niko stood as well. "I will go with her. You and your men are not yet cleared to leave the base."

Stitch grinned. "Well, if you are coming along, you had better move it. It only takes me six minutes to get suited. Meet you at the exterior hatch."

He blinked at the challenge. "So, you will leave without me?"

"Damned straight."

She turned and brought her tray to the drop point. Niko was right behind her.

Long strides had him passing her as she walked down the hall toward her quarters. She didn't rush. She simply unhooked her bra as she walked.

When she was inside her quarters, she stripped and pulled her boots off. The inner liner was hanging in the closet, and it slipped on easily. It was soft and fleecy. She enjoyed using it as pajamas when she needed them.

The outer suit was a tougher skin, and she hopped into it with a wiggle that she thought she had forgotten. Stitch wedged her arms into the sleeves and pulled the suit forward, arching to settle it into place.

A zip, a gel seal to close it and the boots on and she was ready to grab her helmet and go play outside.

She tucked her helmet under her arm and headed for the exterior access, checking on her helmet and the pressure system as she walked.

The breather system provided her with a tank, and she hooked it to her helmet.

Niko skidded into the room and stopped. "How did you get into that suit so fast?"

"Practice. The fashions were a little snug in the capital. I had to get used to using gravity to get me in."

He grinned. "That sounds intriguing. I should try it."

She laughed. "Right. Well, if you are ready, we should get out there."

He called for a charged tank and grabbed his helmet. "Ready when you are."

She put her helmet on, clicked it into place, checked the pressure and read the display. "Can you hear me?"

"Affirmative."

"Any idea which way we should go?"

"Pick a direction. It is all good."

It was less of a direction than she had wanted, but she led the way into the first of the three airlocks.

Each door had a code lock, and she entered her passcode on every pad.

"How do you remember all that?" Niko was right behind her.

"Practice."

They cleared the final lock, and the press of wind made her step back a little. Niko's hands came up to support her.

"Is something wrong?"

She chuckled through their com line. "I just haven't felt the touch of wind in a few years. I forgot how it felt."

She stepped out through the door, and when Niko was through, he closed it. She heard the hiss, but she was too busy staring at the huge planet that they were orbiting and looking at the expanse of greenery with the spikes of volcanoes in the distance.

"Where the hell are we?"

"Alpha Base. It was decided that since the Earth was protected, we should set up a little further afield. We don't know if this place has a name, but we aren't giving it one."

"Where is Omega Base?"

"Another habitable world where they can work on what still needs to be done."

She looked out at the unfamiliar world above her. She could have sworn that they were still near home. She was a little relieved to be wrong.

Her people were safer if the Splice were attacking the cyborgs here.

She walked and scuffed the silver dust of the soil upward. "Can we breathe here?" Her atmospheric readouts were saying yes.

"We don't know what kind of bacteria are in the air. You would be quarantined the moment that you got back to the base."

She nodded. "Right. Well, this is what I wanted to see. Do you mind if I run a little?"

"Feel free. I will keep pace with you."

Stitch nodded and set a goal at what appeared to be a few kilometres away. She started at a light jog before she poured on the speed.

Her interaction with Niko had already turned a little. She could feel his unease, and she was guessing that her strength was what was cooling his jets.

She sighed and kept running. When her oxygen got down close to fifty percent, she turned and started walking back toward Niko. She saw the distance she had covered and upgraded her pace to a light jog.

Niko asked, "Giving up so soon?"

"I use more oxygen than you do. More blood, less metal."

"Right. Should have known that."

She chuckled. "You don't have to. I have to; it is my body that I am dealing with."

"I would like to learn a few of the things that you take for granted."

She drew even with him, and he turned to pace her on the way back to the base.

"Like what? You know a ton of crap that I would never guess at."

"Like what?"

"I have no combat training, can't hit the side of a barn with another barn and have miserable social skills with folks on an even social standing."

"The Alguth have an interest in you."

"Simply because I am the only female and therefore the alpha female on this base. They refer to such females as queens, so I am guessing they have a hive mentality with a prime drone servicing the alpha female."

There was outrage in Niko's voice. "What?"

"Yeah, they engage in competitions to prove who is alpha, and the winner has the best chance with the queen."

"I am going to beat that wingless bastard's ass."

She paused. "Why?"

"Never mind."

She shrugged and returned to jogging

back to the base.

Niko kept at her side. "So, why the running?"

"Because if I do it in the base, folks stare at my ass and boobs the whole time."

He chuckled. "They are fun to watch."

"Perv. I am going to burn it back to the base. Is that a problem for you?"

"Nope, just more fun to watch."

She snorted and put on the speed, watching the metre as the readout slowly dropped and she had five percent of her tank left.

Niko was at her side in seconds, which was good as she had forgotten to take into account the amount of time it would involve to get back into the base.

She entered the code, and when the door opened, they stepped inside. The air was sucked out, and the sterilization kicked in.

She was seeing spots when it came to the second lock, but she made it through.

The second sterilization protocol kicked in, and she was out of oxygen.

"What is it, Stitch?"

"Out of air. Just hold me up, and I will open the lock."

He sighed, and she felt him pin her to the wall while he fiddled with her oxygen unit. He clipped a splitter onto her breather, and she breathed deeply.

He was still pinning her to the wall with his lower body.

"Thanks. I am out of practice."

"You are right. There are things I am better at. It seems that keeping you alive is one of them."

He kept an arm around her, and he entered his own pass code into the pad. They entered the final lock and waited for the scans to confirm they had been scoured.

Niko waited with her until the lights were green and they could enter the base once again. She released the seal of her helmet and inhaled fully.

Niko dropped the used tanks into the recycler and unsnapped the splitter from her helmet.

He picked her up, and she tried protesting.

"I am taking you to medical, Stitch. Any personnel who have had any cognitive dissonance outside the base must report to medical. That currently means you."

"I can walk."

"It is either me or a gurney. Take your pick."

It wasn't that she didn't like being carried; it just wasn't a gesture that she was used to. "I will take you."

He grinned. "Glad to hear it."

When they arrived in the medical centre, Captain Blue was there, and he raised his brows. "Is there something wrong?"

Stitch scowled at him. "No, I just thought that Niko needed the workout."

Niko bounced her a little. "She ran out of oxygen on our way back through the airlocks."

Captain Blue was suddenly all business. "Right. Set her down on the scan table."

Niko set her down, and Captain Blue gave her an injection. He paused. "Oh, damn. I should have had you remove your suit first."

Stitch sighed. "You are enjoying this."

"Only a little. Captain Lukai, if you would help? I am assuming that you have experience getting out of a suit."

He gave Captain Blue a dark look. "Yes, if you give me a sheet for her, that would be appreciated."

Captain Blue suddenly got the expression that she remembered from waking up with him ordering her hand around. He considered her a toy to play with.

He left and got a sheet.

Niko stripped her as efficiently as possible and pulled the sheet over her as soon as it was feasible to do so.

The scan was quick, but Captain Blue actually took on a serious expression when he stared at the results. "What was your previous lung capacity?"

"Not great. I spent years running to increase it. I grew up with serious lung issues."

"Your lungs have been restored to their genetic state. That means that you can't properly exert yourself without passing out. You are just not efficient at processing oxygen. I am amazed that you were admitted to the armed forces."

"I wasn't really. I got along with my mental requirements. That is what was needed, a planner. Someone who could look beyond the wounds and turn them into weapons. The doctors couldn't or wouldn't do it. You should know; I designed you."

He blinked. "What?"

"I was a consultant on your case. I suggested the micro control unit to help you in surgery, and Lucky wrote the program for it."

"Oh. Well, thank you."

"It was my job, and I take my job very seriously."

"Well, due to your genetics, avoid running. Your nanites will keep repairing them to the current state. You will be starting over every day."

She tried to make a fist, and her body slowly reacted.

"Great. Can you flush the paralytic

now?"

"Sure. Of course. If you suffer any more lightheaded episodes, let me know."

He held a small device to her neck, and her hand was released from stricture.

Niko picked her up again and carried her to her quarters.

She rubbed her head. "I just want to rest."

"So, rest. I will be here when you wake."

He tucked her into bed before he peeled off his clothing and crawled into bed with her. He wrapped her in his arms and rubbed his chin along the crown of her head.

She sighed and relaxed in his arms. The time in the machine might have been supposed to keep her up, but her body wanted what it wanted. Right then, it wanted sleep.

Chapter Eleven

"Niko?" She rolled over, and the sheets were cool where he had been lying.

"Well, if he can't be here when I wake up, as he promised, I will just kick him out after sex." She didn't know who she was talking to, but it made her feel better.

She got out of bed and took a shower, towelling her hair dry as she checked her closet. Yup, the liner and her suit were back in place.

She grumbled as she got dressed again. She made her bed and stalked into the base, feeling the eerie quiet the moment she took a step out of her personal space.

She headed to her office instead of stopping for breakfast. The reports were showing two large Splice warships approaching, and so all of the remaining cyborgs had been sent out.

She rubbed her forehead. They had been gone for six hours, and she didn't know how long they were supposed to be gone before she worried.

"Damn it."

"Major Stitch, good morning." Liakon was lounging in her doorway.

"Good morning, Commander Liakon."

"Captain Lukai has given me orders to make sure that you take the time for a meal."

"Good luck with that."

Aluak, the youngest of the Alguth, came in with a tray, and it contained a steaming cup of coffee.

"Well, that is new."

"Captain Lukai also said that delivery was the only way it could be managed."

She sighed as the tray was set on her desk. The hot items were still hot, and the sweet pastry was tucked onto one side.

She sipped at the coffee and sighed.

"Right. I have gotten the specs for your wings, along with a note from Earth Control threatening me with incarceration if I do it. So, we should have the materials on hand to make the struts, I am ordering the machining now. You should be in surgery late this afternoon."

Liakon blinked. "You are risking your own life here?"

"No. Just my freedom. I haven't had much of it so not a huge loss."

She ate with one hand while the other went through the correspondence. She almost missed the note from Windy.

The hidden code nearly skimmed by in a system upgrade. She set her pastry down and got to work.

She dismissed Liakon and sealed the room, putting a com unit into her ear.

The twenty-three-digit code took four tries to get right, but when she heard the familiar voice say, "About fucking time, Stitch," all she could do was laugh.

When she sobered, she said, "It is great to hear your voice, Windy."

"Ah, I do love the old names. So, is it true you have actual aliens running around your base?"

"Damn straight. I just kicked one out. He wants to make me his queen."

Windy snickered. "Who wouldn't? So, what are you up to today?"

"Oh, you know, running around on an alien world, finding out that my adaptation nanites have set me back to the asthmatic wheezer I used to be and waking up to find everybody but the aliens and the med staff off on a mission against the Splice."

"You could always have your lungs removed."

"I really don't want to. There is already less of me than there used to be."

"You and me both, Stitch."

"Have you heard from Alphy or Lacey?"

"Sure. What do you need?"

"More staff."

"If you want more staff, thaw them out. You are sitting on the largest collection of warriors in the galaxy."

She stared at her screens. "What?"

"Sure. Three med officers ago, Alpha Base was made the repository for all off-duty cyborgs. You have them all. The rest of the bases are only to spread out the communications and the administration."

"So, they can't take us all out."

Windy chuckled. "I guess that's the plan."

"It is such a relief to hear you again."

Windy was suddenly sober. "You too. You were the last one back."

The question she had been dreading was now in her throat. "What did they do with the others?"

"Full honours. Fired into the sun."

"Right. Of course."

It was the only way to treat human bodies in space anymore. They had to be burned or they were fodder for the Splice.

There was a pause between them. Windy whispered, "How did we end up like this?"

Instead of giving the canned answer, Stitch answered honestly. "Our people were attacked, we were asked to go as support, and an asshole blew us up because they wanted to surrender to the Splice. Our friends died, we lived and here we are, still trying to support the cause even if we don't know where we are in space."

"Yeah, that sounds about right." Windy chuckled. "If you want a three-way with Cracker, let me know. You have my number."

"Polite dismissal?"

"Yup. I can't hide this signal much longer. Talk to you soon."

The link went quiet, so Stitch put the com headset in her desk and grabbed the file with the specs for the installation of wing struts that would hold the body weight of one of the Alguth.

She brought the designs to medical and showed them to Captain Blue. "Do you think you can manage this?"

"Sure. I will have to check the musculature while I am in there and connect the tendons, but if his body is already re-growing the connections, it will be easier.”

“Great. When do you think you can try this?”

“Well, we have some quiet time now. I can have the parts called up and the team ready in two hours.”

“Excellent. I will tell Liakon to turn up.”

“I have to say, this is a bit exciting. We had no idea they weren’t human when we worked on them.”

“They said they can alter the perceptions of others around them to ensure acceptance.”

“Apparently that is what they did. Their musculature is remarkably similar to ours.”

“I have seen the reports and scans. You aren’t wrong.” She left the reports on his monitor and turned to leave. "See you in two hours."

Now, she just had to find Liakon. She made an educated guess that he would be at the gym.

The Alguth were all working out and chatting with their companions in the way men did when they were trying to relax.

She found Liakon sprinting on a treadmill, and she waved at him.

He turned off the machine and stepped toward her with a weird grace.

"Yes, Major Stitch?"

"Your surgery to implant your wings is in two hours. Just thought you might like to know. Be at medical; I will meet you there."

He was startled. "So soon?"

"Did you want to wait?"

"No. No! This is wonderful."

"Glad you think so. I have more work

to do, but I will meet you there." She patted him on the arm. "Two hours."

He nodded, and there were sparkles of tears in his eyes.

She nodded to the other men in the gym and headed back to the office with a short detour for a cup of coffee and a pastry.

Liakon stripped and lay down on the gurney, she whispered encouragement to him as he was sedated, and she remained outside the surgery with his men while the long spines were grafted to the muscle and tissue in his back.

Solouk whispered, "Major, what do you think the odds of success are?"

"I would say there is a ninety-eight percent chance of success. They have done weirder surgeries with far less chance of success. It should be easy if his musculature has begun to regrow."

She got tired of peering through the window of the surgery and went back to the med bay, bringing up the monitor from the surgical cameras. She and the crowd of Alguth watched as the spines were attached to Liakon's back and the muscles were tested for strength and movement. Wires were used to increase the possible weight load divided across the torso.

They sat and watched as six different struts were attached to different muscle groups.

The aliens were nervous.

Stitch smiled. "Look at the first one."

The new skin was creeping along the metal base, and the silver scales were appearing on the gossamer framework.

She sat in the centre of a bunch of men who were crying with relief.

Wing by wing, the testing for muscle movement proved that Liakon's body controlled the struts.

It took hours for the surgery to go from start to finish, but when Liakon was wheeled out, he was already on his way to wings that were about five feet long.

He was lying on his stomach in recovery, and his men surrounded him.

Stitch sat back and watched as he slowly came out of anaesthesia. He flexed his wings and tried to push himself upward. The med tech pushed his way to his patient's side and coaxed him into lying flat again. He needed a few minutes more.

Stitch watched him slowly come back to normal colour, and his scans gradually cleared, indicating his brain was back online.

The tech helped him sit, and he started fluttering his wings immediately.

Stitch decided to pitch in. The aliens

moved aside for her. "Liakon. Remain calm. Stop trying to move your wings and let the graft take. Tearing out the doctor's work is not going to do you any good. Wait at least three hours, and then, you can start moving."

Aluak smiled. "Can I go next?"

"Let's make sure that they work first, plus let the team recover. We don't have a program to install wings."

Captain Blue came over, looking triumphant but tired. "We have ordered up enough materials for all of you. Two more surgeries and we will have enough data to program the machine."

Stitch pointed to the Alguth. "Keep Liakon from over doing it, and when he can use his wings to fly, you can get in line for the surgery. Not before."

Crystalline webbing was already filling in the spans of the wings. The Alguth were watching his progress with the intensity of folk who were witnessing a miracle.

Stitch returned to her office and got back to work.

Chapter Twelve

It took four hours before Liakon came into her office and fluttered his wings rapidly, lifting off the floor.

"Fine. Coordinate with Captain Blue. He can start a surgical schedule with you."

"You are worried."

"I am. Niko's team has been gone for a while, and I don't know when they are coming back. Yes, I am worried."

Liakon leaned forward. "Do you know where they have gone?"

"Two Splice warships are staging."

"Can you show me where?"

She lowered the lights, and the holo projector showed the Splice ship converging on a planet with three moons.

"Alguth. Look there are other ships coming. We need to be there."

"There is no way to get there. I can't really fly a ship, and I don't have the skills necessary to fight a battle."

He was startled. "I never thought you should come with us."

She smirked. "Like I am going to let a chance like this go by. The moment that the machine is ready, get your men set up and recovering. When they are ready, if there is nothing back from the attack ship, we will head out."

"You are serious? You will take us to the fight?"

"I will take you back to the arms of the Splice. After that, you are on your own. Now, congratulations on your wings, and please, leave me alone. I have to look into the practicalities of this, and I only have seven hours to do it if Captain Blue is willing to do the surgeries."

She waved him off.

The moment he was gone, she grabbed a com unit and called Windy.

"Hiya Windy, sorry to intervene. Have we come up with anything to scuttle a Splice ship yet?"

"Hang on. We are doing that conference call ahead of schedule."

"Sorry. The Splice are targeting a planet and that can't be good."

Windy went quiet while Stitch waited.

"Cracker online."

"Lucky online."

Stitch smiled. "Stitch holding."

The other two chuckled softly.

"Right, since we are all here, I need a means to disable a Splice ship."

Cracker muttered, "That is a rough one. I have designed a spike to get through, but the programming isn't done."

"Yes, it is. I just haven't had a reason to send it to you. The pieces have to come together."

Stitch chuckled. "Well, Lucky, I need it now."

"Data burst on the way. The programming will key the machine to the person who stabs the data notes."

"I will send the design to your manufacturer. Bring as many of them as you can. It will help the infiltrator to take control of the ship."

"The infiltrator being me."

Cracker paused. "The infiltrator being any other cyborg with you. You are irreplaceable, Stitch."

"If that was the case, they wouldn't have left me in the tube for two years."

Lucky cleared her throat. "How long have you been up?"

"Less than a week."

"Oh. Damn. I am sorry, Stitch."

Cracker chipped in. "Schematics have been sent. I have ordered the parts. Did you really give a bunch of aliens their wings back?"

"Yup. Well, we are working on it."

"Wow. What do they look like?"

"Neither the machines nor the doctors could tell them from us. It was the nanites that sent up the flag. I will send you a report on it, Cracker."

"Please. Aliens who look like us. What are the odds?"

"Pretty good considering that the Splice keep looking like generally patchworked people. They seek out a type, and that is why we are here, right? We are around their new tissue source, now that the Earth is out of their reach."

Lucky chuckled. "You could always put the pieces together. Well, take the code, program the spikes and go for it."

"Thanks, ladies. I will be in touch if

this works. If not, watch for a solar flare. Otherwise, I am going to try and do some damage, and we all know that I can manage it if I put my mind to it. Ah well, maybe my guys will return and I won't have to."

"I sent a battle breather design to you that should fit. The manufacturing unit is working on it first."

"So, you guys have been in my computer this whole time?"

Lucky and Cracker muttered, "Pretty much, yeah."

"Glad to know it. These guys need all the help they can get. Okay. Well, good talk. Glad we have all managed this. Now, we just need Alphy and Lacey back in the mix and we will be as complete as we could be."

Windy chuckled. "They are listening, but they don't have active coms. They can hear you."

"Glad you know that you are still out there, ladies. One small step every time and we will finish this."

They all spoke together. "We will finish this."

Winning wasn't an option. There was no win. So many lives lost, humanity torn apart, this wasn't a chance to win, it was a chance to finish the predation.

Unable to leave it on a sombre note, Stitch piped up. "Oh, the Alguth are looking for queens, and the best of their species will fight for the honour to be at your side, so if you have any guys sniffing around and you are going to meet one of the aliens, tell your fellas that they will have some competition."

The ladies were laughing as Stitch disconnected her com and let the sound of feminine laughter warm the cold parts of her mind.

She checked the manufacturing centre, and it was, indeed, working on something small and complex with a huge backlog of copies.

The run would finish in two hours. Until then, it was time to check on the coding.

Lucky was a master. She had produced a code that would not only download all the Splice data, but would also cripple their ship.

Stitch was smiling, and she was almost hoping that the guys were delayed but fine. She really wanted to set foot on a Splice ship with this stuff on her.

She went to the clothing designer and used the specs for the spikes to create a bandolier.

The delivery system was humming with case after case of the spikes.

Time was passing, and the Alguth were beginning to enter the repair machine. There was still no notification from the outgoing ships.

Stitch kept an eye on the processing of the Alguth, and eight hours after her conversation with Liakon, it was time to get into a ship and go in search of the men of Alpha Base.

Every spike that she was wearing was charged with invasive nanites that would do her bidding when it came to taking out a Splice ship. Now, she just had to find the men to help her fly. Her own skills would only take her so far.

She returned to her office with her weapons and cases of spares.

The messages had another encoded line, and it stated, *Look here*. She stared at the text, and a bright flash hit her.

"Ow! Fuckin' Lucky!" She blinked rapidly and held onto the edge of her desk until her vision cleared.

She pinched the bridge of her nose and read the line hidden in the text in front of her. *I know you are a crappy flier. This should help.*

There was information trickling into her mind, and it had to do with piloting spacecraft.

Stitch got to her feet, brought her equipment with her and headed to medical, where the last of the Alguth were coming out of sedation.

Wings were everywhere in different phases of growth.

Liakon came to her and grinned. "We will never be able to thank you."

Stitch pulled him away from the nearest ears. "I believe you will. Will your men freeze in the face of the Splice?"

"No. Now that we are whole, we are ready for a fight."

"Good. I am going to check the ship options, and when I come back, have every man who is ready lined up, dressed and prepared to raid a Splice ship. I want to get my men back."

He nodded. "I will have them ready. Will Captain Blue assist?"

"He had better, or I will have to come back and have a talk with him, and he really doesn't want that today."

Liakon pressed his hand over his heart and bowed.

Stitch took that as agreement and headed to part of the base she hadn't been in before. The hangar.

With wounded in mind, she dialled up the specs on the vehicles still in the hangar. The ship that she selected was the size of a small town, but it would definitely suit her purpose. The guns on it would help her to get where she wanted to go.

She pressed her palm to the authorization plate, and machines went to her choice of vessel to begin the prep for launch. The countdown was on.

Her natural palm was sweating with nerves, but she headed across the hangar on a short-range vehicle until she was next to the huge bulk of the ship. A ladder descended, and she climbed it, entering into the vehicle that would take her into unfamiliar territory.

She stowed the spikes near the cockpit and sat at the controls, running through how to taxi out onto the foreign soil before the ship lifted off.

The weapons array was complicated, but she would have to use her training as best she could.

Stitch swallowed and looked around her, memorizing her territory so that she wouldn't look like she wanted to puke when the Alguth got onboard.

The rear of the ship was set up to carry men, gurneys, outfitted with breathers and weapons. She would be flying an arsenal.

Deep breaths kept her calm as she climbed down the ladder and headed back to the base. She was really going to do this.

Her heart pounded with every step toward medical. She had to hand the base over to Blue. He was next in command.

Captain Blue nodded. "Right. Of course. There is no purpose to this base without what is left of our army. Go and get them, but take Tao. He is an excellent gunner."

Medic Tao was dressed in the light armour and boots of their military. "I was considered to be more valuable as a medic than as a fighter."

Stitch smiled. "I will take all the help I can get."

The Alguth had been kitted out with

light armour and breastplates.

"There are projectile weapons on the ship, so you can arm yourselves before we dock or crash or whatever."

The men looked at each other with slight unease. It made Stitch feel a bit smug as she turned and led her tiny army to the enormous ship.

The *Argon* was ready, and everyone was settled as best they could be, the Alguth standing and holding loops that descended from the ceiling.

Their wings were nearly grown in, but the most recent renovations couldn't be used yet. When they got going, they might just have enough time to get all the guys into full function. Might.

Chapter Thirteen

The hangar was clear of all living personnel when she opened the doors. She moved the ship until it squared up with the opening, and then, the rails they were on helped them trundle ahead.

It was the ultimate in nerve-wracking moments. She had the last point that satellites had sighted the other ship.

The key point was lifting off and setting the computer to follow the path of the sister ship. It was like taking her driver's test to get her skimmer license back home, only way worse.

The ship trundled forward, and she kept her eyes on the clearance of the hangar. The urge was to take off the moment the cockpit cleared, but that would be extremely bad.

Tao was next to her, and he nodded to calm her. "You are doing great, Stitch."

"Thanks. Driving a straight line is my true talent. I have been neglecting it lately."

He chuckled. "This is a brave thing that you are doing, Stitch. Don't let that freak you out."

She snorted. "I wasn't, until now. Thanks for that."

He laughed, and they cleared the hangar. The huge doors shut, and it was now or never. She released the docking clamps that held the ship down and got ready.

Stitch powered the jets up and took a stabilizing breath before she hit the elevation controls, and the jets pushed them upward. The ship shuddered until she got a handle on it, and then, it was a smooth pull upward.

The blackness of space was a huge relief. She had been afraid that she forgot to pull the landing gear in.

A quick check of the controls told her that they were up and out of the atmosphere.

"You did it, Stitch."

His voice was familiar. "Tao, you had a central core injury. You got scorched."

He chuckled. "You remember! I thought that you only recognized the fighters."

"No, I recognize voices, and this is the first time we have spoken. If I can't see your wounds, your voice is the only way I would recognize you as one of the men I met."

She programmed in the coordinates she had been given, letting the computer do the calculations to compensate for orbital motion.

With a sigh of relief, she sat back as the ship's controls took over.

Her hands were trembling, both silver and natural. "And now, we are on our way, and I need a cup of coffee."

She walked down the steps, waved at the Alguth and informed them, "We are cruising and should be at the attack point in four hours. Time for a snack and a cup of coffee."

They followed her down to the galley, and everyone lined up at the dispensers. It was nice to see that they had settled in.

She got a solid lunch and a cup of coffee along with a few bags of water. She remembered breather training; she was going to need to brush her teeth before she put it on.

When she sat at a table, the Alguth surrounded her.

Liakon asked, "What are we supposed to do?"

She blinked. They were all looking at her for guidance. *Fuck.*

"I need you to go in, find our men and any of yours that are penned up or caged. Even those that are being used for parts. You know what we can do. Bring them home, and we will try to get them back in time to insure their survival."

Liakon nodded and sighed in relief.

"Kill any Splice that you come across. We are not here for negotiations; we are not here for hostages; we are here to get our men back."

Liakon nodded, and his grin was feral. "We can do that."

"Good. While you do that, I am going to find every data port I can find and jam a spike into it. With luck, I can get at least half a dozen of them, which is what we need to crack their system.”

Solouk scowled. “You are doing this alone?”

“I am a crappy fighter. I can’t hit any-thing with a weapon. My skills lie in analysis. I have to be here, because there isn’t another person at the base that can be spared. If I die, it won’t be the end of the project. The guys can fly this beast home.”

The men were shocked.

She ate her food and tried not to think about it as it went down. Travel rations were not the best.

The coffee washed her food down, and the Alguth were speaking in their language as they ate their own meals.

Aluak took her tray when she was done and left her with the water.

The men continued to talk around her, and she sighed, took her water and headed up to the command deck.

Tao left and took his own turn at his break.

Stitch watched the stars around them and the speed increasing as they continued to accelerate toward their destination.

She sipped at her water and watched the data links to satellites flare as they cruised through space.

It was an hour before Tao returned, and he was shaking his head. "The Alguth have assigned you a bodyguard. Aluak will be at your side during the attack on the ship."

"Oh. Goody. Did they give you a reason as to why?"

"They don't want their queen dying in battle."

She groaned. "I am not their queen, and I don't intend to die."

"Tell them, not me. They are planning the fastest hit they can manage to get you back to the ship with the utmost speed."

"Lovely. I look forward to it." She chuckled.

Time went by quickly, and she spent her time trying to decide if she wanted to go left or right.

When the scanners caught the ships at long distance, she had to decide fast.

"Let's look for life signs." Tao ran the scanner with practice, and she sighed in relief. Finally, she could leave one decision to someone else.

"I have them. They are on the ship on the left. The one further away. If we pass the one on the right, we are going to have a fight on our hands."

"That is why you are here, Tao."

He grinned. "I will try and take out their command deck."

"Good. If you manage it, I will try and think of a suitable reward."

"I will settle for a kiss from you."

"That I can deliver. It isn't regulation, but then, neither am I."

"Wonderful. It's a deal." He winked and pulled the gunner's rig toward him.

He was sighting, and she realized that she had better get them in close while still aiming for the other ship.

She took control of the ship and prepared for the manoeuvers.

"The Splice command deck is on the top of the ship, in the rear. Bring us in."

She had the target, so she brought them in.

The whir of the guns echoed in the ship as they drew closer. When the Splice weapons began to target them, Tao took aim and blasted the weapons first before aiming at the command deck.

The Splice ship jerked and veered to one side.

"Got it."

"Great, aim at the other one; we are coming in a little too fast."

She fired the braking engines carefully, and while Tao blasted the weapons on the ship, she locked the *Argon* to the side of the Splice ship and triggered the boring lock.

"Honey, we're home." She smiled and got out of her seat, getting her bandolier and putting the rest on a belt. She had her data spikes loaded with nanites, and she was ready.

She really hoped she was ready.

She put the breather on and gestured for the Alguth to do the same. They all kept their breathers on, and when the filtered air hit them, they smiled. Splice ships stank.

The boring lock was ready, and the initial Alguth warriors prepared to fire.

They exited the lock, blew the boring lock in, and the explosive knocked back the Splice that had gathered in the hall.

Gunfire began, and Aluak stuck to her side as they followed the other fifteen into the Splice ship.

It wasn't great that those men had been held captive, but they did know where to go.

The first com node that she saw, she drove the spike in deep. It lit up and fired up.

The bodies of the Splice lined the halls, their patchwork limbs made her gag. None of the pieces belonged to the same species, and it was disturbing.

When she saw an Earth military tattoo, she gritted her teeth to stop her from sobbing. The next spike went into another node.

Aluak was an excellent bodyguard. He kept a few steps ahead of her and cleared a path, recharging the projectiles and the charged weapons alike.

They kept working toward the command deck, and she had punched eight of the spikes into the nodes when they found a lab.

Stitch stumbled into the room, and she found Nikolai pinned to the wall, cut and bloody. The steel shafts pinned his adaptations to the wall.

Stitch grabbed his arm next to the steel invader, and she pulled his arm away from the wall. She pulled his legs loose one by one, and then, she yanked his final arm free.

He leaned heavily on her, and Aluak offered, "Give him to me. We have to get out of here."

She grunted and handed her unconscious man to Aluak.

She couldn't shoot their way out, but she could fight.

With Aluak moving toward the bore-hole, she backed him up. When a Splice appeared, hissing and muttering in whatever language it was that they spoke, she drew back her fist and punched it through his skull.

A second attacker tried to lunge for her, but he grabbed one of the spikes. He drove it into her arm, and she hissed as the communication nanites ran into her system.

"Fuck."

She punched his skull into crushed and smashed pieces with her wounded arm.

Her mind lit up with knowledge of the location of everything on the ship. She wrapped her thoughts in control and sent the ship on a trajectory that would take it into the sun.

"We have to move, boys."

The crowd that was waiting for them

on the *Argon* was full of unfamiliar faces, and many blissfully familiar ones.

Aluak took Nikolai to the med bay, and the rest were settled in the transport seats.

She asked Tao, "How bad are the wounds?"

"Not too bad. They were more interested in torture for information. We only lost one man."

"Who?"

"Elmer Theric. He didn't speak much and was rather shy."

"Right, well we need to get away from this ship. It is on its way to its doom. Now, I need to get into the next one."

"Why? It is crippled."

"I can destroy it, and wouldn't that be better?"

Aluak returned and nodded. "I will accompany you again."

"Fine. Bring more guns. We won't

have to get in as far, but we still need six nodes."

Aluak nodded. "The best collection would be the command deck. Multiple nodes in one room."

"That sounds like a plan to me."

She smiled and ran back to the command deck to direct them into position.

They bored into the hold, and everyone planted the spikes with only nine dead Splices to show for it. The data was removed and sent from the ship, and she used her control to aim it to the sun.

Aluak looked up. "They have my people on board."

"Aw fuck. Let's get them."

She picked up Splice weaponry with the knowledge of how to use it coming through the data linkage.

"Now, Aluak."

They ran through the halls, shooting their way to the labs and holding pens full of Alguth.

She guarded her collection of aliens as they were ushered through the hall, back to the breech point. Aluak kept them calm and kept them running. Several still had their original wings.

When they were back on board the *Argon,* she was covered in blood, hers and the Splices'. She confirmed the locked-in programming that would send the large ship to the sun and released the lock before setting a course for home.

Chapter Fourteen

Flying home with a ship full of folks needing help was a nightmare. She sent a data burst and hoped Captain Blue was reading his mail.

Her list was detailed as to what was needed for Earth military and the Alguth.

She really needed a nap, but the ship had gone from being extremely empty to full capacity.

"So, you sent both of those ships into the sun?"

"I did. They will hit sometime in the next hour; their engines are on full, so I hope that Windy is quick with the download."

Stitch jerked when a voice whispered in her mind, *I am on it.*

She looked to Tao. "Did you hear that?"

He scowled at her. "No. You should get that looked at."

She flexed her hand and looked at the hole closing up. "It's fine."

"Are you sure; you look a little weird."

"I feel fine. Is everyone stable?"

"They are."

"Then, let's punch it."

She set course for home and accelerated.

The moment the ship had control, she got up and headed to the cargo hold where the wounded were being taken care of.

She knelt next to Niko and looked him over. His nanites were healing his wounds, but they would need more mass to continue the repairs.

She stroked his head and kissed his lips softly. She felt his hand touch the back of her head and hold her as the kiss grew intense.

She laughed and carefully straddled his torso. "So, you are feeling better."

There was a small smile on his lips. "Where are we?"

"The cargo hold of the *Argon*. I got worried, so I grabbed the men I could, and here we are."

"Thank goodness for your instincts. We were ambushed. The second ship was playing dead."

"Where did your ship end up?"

"Crashed on the planet. They shook it off, and gravity took over."

"Fuck." She pressed her hands to his shoulders and checked for damage with slow caresses.

"If this is what you are like with the wounded, I think I am going to have to start supervising."

He stroked her ribs and back, so his arms were working again.

"One of your legs is broken. It will have to be replaced at the base."

He nodded. "I can feel it."

"So, they were out for information?"

"Yes, the Alguth are an easier tissue source than we are, so they wanted to know what we did with the ones that we took."

"What did you tell them?"

"Nothing. They were only getting started. I applaud you on your timing."

"Major, we need help!" Aluak was holding a young man down, and he was thrashing.

The damage to the Alguth's body was intensive. Stitch got to her feet and grabbed the nearest med kit.

The outline of the explosive device was unmistakable. "Aw, fuck."

George was nearby, and he was coming toward her with a bomb box. Another survivor was prepping a cold tube.

"Aluak, he has a bomb inside him. Things are going to happen quickly. I am going to sedate him, remove the bomb, inject the primer nanites and he will be put into the cold tube to keep him alive."

"A bomb?"

"Explosive device. You know." While she worked, she prepped the injectors and tried to keep calm. The Splice had created a large incision to create the space in the man's torso. This was not a small bomb.

"George, are you ready to flush the box as soon as I get this out?"

"Standing by, Stitch."

As the only perfectly healthy crewman, it was her duty to do this. If Tao hadn't been in command, she would have had him do this, but the detonation sequence of the bomb wasn't a known quantity.

Best to get it out and launch it.

"Are you ready?"

Aluak held the young man down. Another Alguth held his feet. She grabbed the first hypo, injected him several times around the wound, grabbed the second to sedate him, and the moment his eyes fluttered closed, she used her silver hand to pull open his wound and grab the bomb.

"Coming out." The wet, sucking sound of the bomb leaving the young man was nauseating, but she pulled it free and dropped it in the box.

The box was closed, and George ran to the disposal, dumping the bomb box with a hiss and a clank.

The moment she was free of the bomb, she grabbed two nanite primers and struck the young man with them as his body shivered and started to buck. She didn't want to know yet what they had removed to make room for the explosive.

"Right. Cold tube."

Aluak and the other man lifted the young man and tucked him in the tube. With bloody hands, Stitch set the controls and the racing pulse slowed to barely perceptible but stable.

George was already scanning the others, and while a few trackers were found and launched, there were no other bombs.

She returned to Niko's side and smiled. "Did they put anything in you?"

"Just the spikes. Our nanites would break them down quickly."

She stroked his face again, and he smiled.

"I love it when you do that."

"Why?" She continued to touch his

familiar features before placing her hands over his heartbeat, feeling the reassuring thud.

"It shows that you forgive me for taking off on you."

"Duty called. I can let that one slide." She chuckled. "Well, I have to get back to the command deck. I am flying this thing."

She kissed him quickly and left him with the others lying in various conditions. All stable but few were mobile.

Hours of flight were ahead of her, but she was bringing her guys back.

The med teams signalled standby as she landed, and there was a sigh of relief.

She glanced over at Tao as she set the ship down and snickered. "You can uncover your eyes now."

He grinned and dropped his hand as the docking rails started pulling them back into the hangar.

The moment the hangar doors closed and the area was filled with scrubbed air, the med team started streaming toward them.

She looked at Tao. "We did it."

He grinned. "We did; now, get your ass to medical for scans."

"Yes, Medic."

She grabbed her remaining collection of spikes and headed down to assist in getting the wounded into the base.

If the communications from Earth Control could have shot lasers, they would have. She typed the reports out, including the Splice's alternate tissue source in the Alguth and filled in that this was a less advanced species than humans and asked permission to assist the Alguth in their defense of their own world.

When the response came, she was sitting in recovery, chatting with the new cyborgs. Their stabilizing surgeries had been done, and more of the forty men rescued were still in line to get their work done. She had already spent time in pre-op.

The message ripped into her mind, and she gasped. "What the fuck?"

Major Carter, you are relieved of duty. The new species is on their own. We will not squander our resources on men and women not our own if there is no obvious gain.

There was more data and even more insults to the Alguth, but she got the gist of it.

She patted the knee of the man who was looking at her with concern.

"I have to go see Captain Nikolai. Excuse me."

The men made sounds that indicated

disappointment, but as charming as it was, she needed to talk to Nikolai.

He was in the secondary pre-op, waiting with his men to help them into the machine.

"Niko, do you have a moment?"

He set one of his guys into the machine, and he nodded.

"Can we go somewhere private?"

"I prefer to remain here. Styo hasn't been in the machine before."

She could see his point. "Well, I have been relieved of duty, and Earth Control has ordered us to expel all Alguth from our premises. They are refusing to assist them."

"Fuck them."

"That is my thought as well. Did you know we are sitting on a small army?"

"What?"

"More cyborgs in storage under our feet. The sublevels under our feet have about fifteen hundred wounded men who have been rebuilt."

Niko's shock was on his face and in every line of his body.

"That would be enough to outfit every ship we have. We could strike at the Splice and take out several of their mother ships."

"What do you recommend?" She bit her lip. She had an idea.

He narrowed his eyes. "What are you thinking, Stitch?"

"Well, since Earth is safe and we are cut off from them, why not see if the Alguth will let us set up a base on their world and we can deploy from there."

His smile was slow; he pulled her into him by virtue of a hand around her waist. "I love the way your mind works. Are you serious about the hidden army?"

"I am. I think it was the final reserve."

"Do you know where they are?"

She grinned. "As soon as Styo is out and you are willing to go exploring, I will show you. The schematics are hidden in the system."

He kissed her, pressing her against the wall and holding her in place with his body. She wrapped her legs around him and returned the embrace. Their kiss became heated, and he ran his hands over her battle suit. A light tapping on the interior of the machine behind them eventually brought them out of it. Styo wanted out.

George took over shepherding the cyborgs in for repair.

Stitch and Niko walked the halls with heads high and chatting neutrally. They went past the gym, past the dining hall and into the hangar. Stitch mentally chanted the authorization code, and when they made their way beneath the scaffolding and walkways, she found the access panel.

The numbers and letters took her thirty seconds to key in.

Niko didn't rush her.

When the door opened, she dropped into the hatch, skidding down the steps by hanging onto the railing and letting gravity take her down.

Niko dropped in behind her.

She stepped away from the ladder, looking for the switch to turn on the lights, and Niko echoed her inhalation.

He wrapped his arms around her and he murmured, "There has been an army asleep under our feet the whole time."

"I am getting a funny feeling about this."

"What?" He pressed a kiss to her neck, and it was an effective distraction.

She turned and kissed him while stroking a hand down his chest. There was no one around to interrupt, and they were hidden in this high-security vault.

"Why, Major Carter, are you making an advance on me?"

She cupped his obvious erection. "Should I make a joke about inappropriate weaponry?"

He laughed harshly and pulled at her clothing until her pants were at mid-calf and his hand could find its way into her wet folds.

"It seems you are ready for me." He pressed his lips to her neck.

"Just put me up against the wall and fuck me. I am really tired of giving orders."

She had polished, cold metal at her back and he was between her thighs with only a few rough fumbles.

Stitch gasped and dug her hands into his shoulders.

Niko ran his tongue over her neck,

and he thrust his hips upward, jerking her onto him. He moved a hand under her shirt and squeezed her breast as he began to hammer upward with steady beats.

The slick slide of his cock inside her increased her pleasure, and the rough handling sent her over the edge far faster than she wanted. She hissed through clenched teeth as her body wrapped around him, and he shoved into her in time to her body's frantic clutching.

He groaned against her throat, and the sound echoed in her mind. She threaded her fingers through his hair and pulled his head up for a kiss.

His cock twitched inside her as she pulsed around him again.

"I wasn't afraid of the Splice; I was afraid I wouldn't see you again."

She sighed against his lips. "I led a group of aliens and a medic after two

Splice warships because you didn't wake me to say good bye."

He chuckled. "We are a pair."

"Yeah, we are. I need to put my pants back on now."

"I like being inside you; you are so tight."

She blushed. "Right, well, you would be the authority on that."

He grinned and bent his knees. Slowly pulling out of her as she ended on her feet and he was crouching.

"Back up a step." She gave him a look. "Why?"

"I don't want to get hit in the head with your cock on the way down or up."

He chuckled and stepped back as he tucked his relaxing erection into his trousers.

She wiggled her way into her underwear and made a face at the damp sensation as she snugged her pants onto her hips.

"That is an incredible face you are making right now."

"Dealing with my cum and yours makes walking distinctly uncomfortable."

"I would say I am sorry, but now, I just want to get you into a shower."

"Well, Niko, as you are now the commanding officer again, you need to know this. Let's go exploring."

"I thought that was what we just did."

She grinned and grabbed his hand, hauling him along. "That was a condensed version of greatest hits."

He was chortling when they reached the end of the dark hall and they didn't need the light switch.

Over a thousand deep-cold chambers were lined up in groupings that didn't seem to have any rhyme or reason.

She left Niko and headed down, off

the viewing walkway, and she headed for the back of the storage area.

"When I was with my family, there was a file about previous research into cyborgs."

"I thought the Carters were the founders of the cyborgs."

"Only the current generations. The ones that are just men, adaptations and nanites."

She stopped next to one of the containers and brought up the medical file. She put her hand over her mouth and swallowed.

"What? You look like you just saw a ghost."

She turned to stare at him. "How long has this base been here?"

"Eight years."

She went through the modules, looking frantically for something familiar.

She pressed her forehead to the tube

when she found him.

"Who is it? Your lover?"

She turned her head and smiled weakly at him. "This is my elder brother, Lexo. He was a first volunteer and one of the first generation of cyborgs. They made him into a weapon, and then, they put him away like a broken toy."

"What was so special about the first generation? We are all built for battle."

"They aren't built for battles. They are weapons. Arms, legs, everything has weapons built in. Killing is their only purpose."

Niko looked at her and then back to the man in the canister. "Well, fuck."

She couldn't add anything to that.

Chapter Fifteen

Sitting in the command office, Niko asked, "What do you want to do?"

"I want to ask the Alguth if they want help, and if so, I want to return their fighters to them."

"If the Alguth want to go."

"Right. That. I think they do."

She finally managed to crack the roster of the men in cold sleep.

"Holy crap. The Sisters are down there as well."

Niko looked over her shoulder. "What are the Sisters?"

"Females who volunteered to be made into medical cyborgs. They were also given programming that went a little wrong."

"What was it?"

"The women were programmed as sexual companions to all comers, so to speak."

"It sounds a little rough but not horrible."

"Their program got them to feel pleasure all the time, any touch, any sensation, it all got them off."

Niko frowned. "Your voice says it isn't a good thing."

"Put someone who feels pleasure at every stimuli into a combat situation, and then, what do you have when the fight is over?"

"Oh, shit."

"Yeah, it was a short project and why women weren't supposed to be on the front lines." She gave him a dark glance. "The women in the basement are sexy and exceptionally dangerous. If we do wake up that army, we have to do it one at a time."

"So, what do we do next?" Niko's knee was touching her own.

"First thing is to ask the Alguth if they want to go home. I can fly them. "

"Right. Like I will let that happen."

She poked him in the chest. "You are not the boss of me. You read the memo. I am a mascot only."

He grabbed her finger and sucked it into his mouth, swirling his tongue around it.

She shivered and felt her eyes droop heavily. Her hair was still damp from her shower, and she slowly pulled her finger out of his mouth. "Don't tease. This is serious."

"It wasn't a tease. It was an invitation."

She raised her brows and climbed into his lap. "Well, in that case, who do you want to talk to first? The men or the Alguth?"

"I think that we should get everyone together. This isn't something that I want to get into if everyone isn't on board."

She stroked his neck, and he looked down at her. In a high falsetto, she said, "You are so smart."

"You are one second away from being dumped off my lap."

She laughed and got to her feet. "Everybody needs to be included. Even me."

He grinned and got to his feet, calling for a base-wide meeting to be held in medical in half an hour. Attendance was mandatory.

So, Stitch, you are really doing this.

Why the fuck can I hear you, Windy?

The communication nanites went straight to your brain. Plenty of room in there.

Funny. And weird. So, what do you want?

If you can get a new base on Alguth, you won't be alone. Earth Command has cut us off. We need a place to go, and it looks like the Alguth need defending. If they are interested, we can swing by and help grab your sleeping cargo.

I am going to have to engage in politics, and we all know that it isn't my forte.

If you want a place on Alguth, Alphy will be only too happy to step into the breach.

Tell her to do whatever it is that she can to gain us a site on Alguth. We will go there, bodies ready and weapons hot.

Excellent. I am passing it along. I will let you know when the Alguth reply.

Oh, and we have fifty-five of their

men *that are repaired and ready to fight.*

I am grabbing the files from your computers. Anything she can show them will be helpful, I am sure.

Okay, I have to go; the meeting is in half an hour. I have never planned a mutiny before. This is going to get weird.

The only way you do it. Have a fun mutiny, Stitch.

Windy went silent, and Stitch shook her head as if to dislodge the voice.

"What was that?"

She winked. "I will explain it when we are naked. It will be funnier."

"Tempting, but it will have to wait until later. Are you ready?"

"Yup. I am already out of this party. I am just here to watch."

He sighed. "You know just what to say to distract the hell out of me."

"Excellent. I am going to need a new job."

"It only has a few benefits." He was walking slightly ahead of her, so she grabbed his ass. He jumped and turned to her in shock.

"So far I like the ones I can lay hands on."

"You are going to be a pain in the ass, aren't you?"

"Only if I start pinching. Come on. Serious meeting to hold about engaging in mutiny and trying to get the Alguth back to their people."

She shooed him along, and he gave her a black look over one shoulder. They headed to medical, and the room was rapidly filling with humans and their alien guests.

Stitch watched as Niko stood on an exam table and started to explain the situation with Earth Command and the

Alguth.

After he was done, George called out, "Stitch, what do you think?"

"I have been relieved of duty for insubordination. So, technically not allowed to influence those of you who want to remain under the umbrella of Earth Command."

She smiled calmly and stood at ease.

The vote was shockingly unanimous. Since they had no chance of returning home, putting roots down with the Alguth were as good as it was going to get. They would help defend against the Splice.

It was a relief and oddly freeing for the men who had been obsessed with the duty to the base.

"Right, so we are going to do this."

The men cheered.

Stitch looked to Niko, and he pulled her up to stand next to him.

"Okay. So, we are still the military, wear what you want in your off hours as long as you wear something. On duty, on missions, everybody remember that we are representing humanity out here. We are unified, and we will fight for our two species' survival." She put her silver fist in the air. "With a mechanical advantage!"

The cheer confused the Alguth, but they greeted their new unit mates with handshakes and pats on the shoulder. It was all very grownup and masculine.

Niko looked down at her. "Did we just do that?"

"I think we did. Are you ready to rob this place blind and move house?"

He looped his arms around her waist and grinned. "I don't know. Moving in together is a big step."

"Moving in?"

"Well, we will have to create plans

once we find the next source for our base. That will involve many late nights, and of course, we will still need to fight the Splice when they get in close."

"So, you want to move in together and live... together?"

Liakon snorted from nearby and said, "You two draw each other. Even I can see it, as much as I wish it was other-wise."

Stitch looked at him and narrowed her eyes. "Quiet, you. I was getting the ass end of a proposal here."

Niko knelt at her feet. "Let me make it formal. Would you, Stephanie Carter, do me the honour of sharing a domicile with me with an eye toward a permanent bond?"

She grinned. "You just want to jump my bones whenever convenient."

"That is correct."

A wave of laughter moved through

the men.

She stroked his face, and he closed his eyes, leaning into her hand. "Of course. Consider it an engagement and the present that you seal it with can be a place to live."

He lifted her and hopped from the table, hugging her and twirling her around.

Stitch held onto him with all her strength, surrounded by their motley group, and she hoped that this was going to have a happy ending for all. She knew it wouldn't, but for now, hope was the best four-letter word in her lexicon.

Conference season looms, so I can be found at RT in Las Vegas (April), RTC in Ottawa (May), and RAGT in June (Ohio).

This means a delay until July for book two of this six-book series, but it will be there, the cyborgs will be back, and we will see where the other five survivors have been. Well, we will see the story of one of them.

Thanks for reading,

Viola Grace

About the Author

Viola Grace (aka Zenina Masters) is a Canadian sci-fi/paranormal romance writer with ambitions to keep writing for the rest of her life. She specializes in short stories because the thrill of discovery, of all those firsts, is what keeps her writing.

An artist who enjoys a story that catches you up, whirls you around and sets you down with a smile on your face is all she endeavours to be. She prefers to leave the drama to those who are better suited to it, she always goes for the cheap laugh.